THE
ARCHITECTURE
OF DESIRE

ALSO BY MARY GENTLE

A Hawk in Silver
Golden Witchbreed
Ancient Light
Scholars and Soldiers
Rats and Gargoyles

MARY GENTLE

THE ARCHITECTURE OF DESIRE

 VIKING / A ROC BOOK

VIKING/ROC
Published by the Penguin Group
Penguin Books USA Inc., 375 Hudson Street,
New York, New York 10014, U.S.A.
Penguin Books Ltd, 27 Wrights Lane,
London W8 5TZ, England
Penguin Books Australia Ltd, Ringwood,
Victoria, Australia
Penguin Books Canada Ltd, 10 Alcorn Avenue,
Toronto, Ontario, Canada M4V 3B2
Penguin Books (N.Z.) Ltd, 182–190 Wairau Road,
Auckland 10, New Zealand

Penguin Books Ltd, Registered Offices:
Harmondsworth, Middlesex, England

Published by Viking/Roc, an imprint of New American Library,
a division of Penguin Books USA Inc. Originally published in
Great Britain by Bantam Press.

First Viking/Roc Printing, March, 1993
10 9 8 7 6 5 4 3 2 1

LIBRARY OF CONGRESS CATALOGING IN PUBLICATION DATA
Gentle, Mary.
    The architecture of desire / Mary Gentle.
        p.   cm.
    ISBN 0-451-45234-8
    I. Title.
PR6057.E525A89   1993
823'.914—dc20   92–23996
                                          CIP

Printed in the United States of America
Set in Caledonia and Benguiat

We had fed the heart on fantasies,
The heart's grown brutal from the fare

—W. B. Yeats
Meditations in Time of Civil War, VI

CONTENTS

I

"But I don't understand *why* the servants have to form a collective," the Lord-Architect said plaintively.

His huge bulk shifted as he leaned back, swivel-chair creaking, and prodded a fat finger into the air.

"*And* I don't see why they have to eat at the same table that we do!"

Winter light shone through the tall windows, slotting down from the glass cupola onto his tilted drawing-table. A smell of heat and sea-coal filled the immense room. A draught chilled his stockinged calves. Morning whiteness illuminated high ceilings; plaster-mouldings; walls covered in plans, drawings, charts of tensile strength; and the T-square and tracing-board hung up over the Adams fireplace.

"In addition to which," he added, with dignity, "I have more important matters to consider."

"Oh, listen to him!"

A plan scrolled up, rattling, as he took his bolster-heavy elbow off it. He scowled. "Rot it!"

The White Crow grinned. She added: "I can think of at least one good reason why they should. Hazelrigg and the rest have been indentured here for the past forty years; the

9

last time *I* saw the place I was hardly older than Jared; and
I know as much about farming and estate-management as
you do about—about, for example, music!"

The Lord-Architect appeared hurt. "I can sing."

"Mmm. One could say you have a way with music. One
could say King Herod had a way with children."

The White Crow sprawled back in the deep armchair.
In her right hand, awkwardly, she held a blackletter pam-
phlet. Six or seven other pamphlets rested across her lap.
Her studded brown leather doublet and lace-linen shirt
unbuttoned, she cradled a baby in the crook of her left
arm while it suckled at her bare breast. She divided her
time between reading and beaming aimlessly into the mid-
dle-distance.

"It's bloody Elias Ashmole again!" One-handed, she brandished a sheaf of papers. "Here's Lilly in *The Starry Messenger,* and Ashmole in *The White King at Liberty,* and damned
if they haven't dragged that fool Aubrey in. The next thing,
we'll have John Evelyn and the whole Astrologers' Observatory putting out this rubbish! This war's gone on for years,
thank you very much, and it isn't going to stop for the
prophecies of a couple of fifth-rate astrologers. I'm going
to have to get up to London and collect the next lot of
pamphlets."

"I've got it!" Oblivious of her, the Lord-Architect Casaubon dipped his index finger into the inkwell and began to
smudge in shadows on the full-frontage drawing. The furred
hem of his wide sleeve trailed through the standish.

"What did I tell you!" His fat finger stabbed the col-
umns of figures on papers that slid rustling to the carpet.
"A *direct* correlation—the fewer floors on any tenement,
the fewer snatch-purses working the building. The fewer
corners for nips and foists to hide and spy out victims. If
the number of walkways is cut, then *down* goes the number of Abraham-men and silver-priggers. Design it with
no more than one entrance to a courtyard, there's but one

way out past the Watch—and your thief goes a-looking for some other ken."

He rubbed his wide forehead absently with his finger, smearing ink across copper-red brows.

"Let me rebuild the St. Sophia Rookeries and I'll have their thievery and thuggery down by nine-tenths in a year. It's perfect!"

"*Now* all you have to do is persuade the Protector to let you do it." She paused, her sardonic gaze vague.

"It would drastically lower the crime-rate . . . little one?"

"Every faction has to have its astrologers," the White Crow finished morosely, "and they're going to catch up with me sooner or later."

"Sooner," the Lord-Architect hazarded.

"*Thank* you, Casaubon."

She absently dropped a kiss on her child's hair. Bright enough red to be orange, the hair curled in tiny, damp sweat-rings. The smell of milk and baby clung to her fingers along with the printer's ink.

"Regarding the collective—I say what I said at thirteen." The White Crow shifted the baby in her arm. Her index finger stroked the child's lip and her own breast. "If I *wanted* to run a hotel-sized kitchen, or enough staff to keep a city parish in order, or be landlord to four farms, then I'd have *asked* to do so."

The light barred her face, calling out fire from her dark red brows, and citrine light from her irises.

"To which I add now: why shouldn't the whole lot belong to the people who work it? I don't. God He knows my family never did."

The Lord-Architect raised a brow at her, appalled. "Mad. Completely mad."

He witnessed her expression of disquiet, as if panelled walls and high, bright ceiling and the blazing fire rebuked her. She rallied:

"*And,* if we don't eat at the same table, you won't get to

hear gossip about Hazelrigg's mistress. Or how the work's going, down at the excavations. Or what Rowland's sister wrote to him about news in town. Nor will you be able to collapse young Denzil with what I, for one, regard as fairly feeble wit. True?"

In tones of injured dignity, Casaubon protested, "That is hardly the point!"

She let the pamphlets slide to the floor, sitting up to put the child in the bassinet. The open hearth-fire roared hollowly at her back. The White Crow hitched up her belt and leather breeches and walked across to the windows. Her boots, soundless on rugs, scraped the scrubbed pine boards. She leaned both hands against the window. Her breath fogged the cold glass.

"It isn't as bitter as yesterday. *Told* you it was going to snow."

A yellow light emanated from the cloud-cover, the sky lighter than the east wing's roofs and the forest beyond the grounds. Black specks showed against it. Below, white clots of snow feathered down the air to skein the earth.

Baltazar Casaubon, Lord-Architect, tugged his fingerless gloves on more securely. He scratched at his short, copper-red hair, flicking scurf from under his nails. He picked up his goblet of mulled wine and cupped it with both large hands for warmth.

"When I ruled my own city, servants knew their place!"

"Firstly, it wasn't your city; secondly, it's a republic these days, and no great wonder; thirdly—"

The Lord-Architect interrupted: "Why aren't you wearing your sword?"

The woman swore.

Her voice echoed the length of the long room, sharp in the cold air. She turned from the window and marched to his table.

Casaubon sat back, startled. Standing at the back of the tilted drawing-table, she was tall enough to rest her arms on it, and her chin on her arms, and gaze at him. Faint lines contracted round her narrowed eyes. Studs glinted in her brown leather doublet; lace fell crisp from collar and cuffs.

"I apologise," she said sweetly, "for mention of the word *Republic.*"

The Lord-Architect slammed down his goblet of mulled wine. Rivulets spilled down onto the sleeves of his velvet robe; trickled down the scrolled paper, the table, and onto the furred hem of his gown.

He wiped his mouth. "What sort of a Scholar-Soldier can you call yourself, and not wear a sword?"

He tugged the voluminous green velvet gown more tightly over the shirt and breeches that strained to encompass his stomach, and climbed massively down from the chair. Rolls of flesh shifted. From his full height of six feet, five inches, he looked down at her over the swell of chins, chest, and belly, reaching a sticky finger to her cheek.

"Little one . . ."

Cold made her skin pale, lucid under dark red hair drawn up in the Scholar-Soldiers' six braids. He touched softness. At each of her temples, and no larger than his thumbprint, a patch of white down-feathers grew: sleek, soft, merging into the white streaks of her hair.

She caught his fingers, pressing the padded, dirty flesh to her cheek. "You weren't born to understanding servants. True enough. Yes. I should remember. No, really, you're doing *very* well."

The Lord-Architect stamped one stockinged foot. "Death and furies! I will not be condescended to in my own house."

"*Whose* own house?"

Deadpan, and with quick calculation, he reprised. "I will not be condescended to in your own house!"

He almost had her: her mouth twitched.

One of the room's double doors clicked open. A stocky fair-haired boy, perhaps eight years old, entered and reached up to the ornate handle, pushing the door closed behind him. He pulled at the turned-back cuffs of his diminutive frock-coat.

"Mama, Hazelrigg says you had better come to the yard-gate."

"In this weather?" Casaubon remarked. Through the glass, on the terrace, snow whitened the flagstones to invisibility.

The White Crow began absently to button up her shirt and doublet. "Why does he want me, Jared?"

"Mama, he says there's a troop of mercenary soldiers just riding onto the estate."

The White Crow clattered down steps into a stone-floored kitchen, ducking her head to avoid hanging hams and pheasants. Fumbling, fingers paralysed with cold, she slid sideways between the grain-bins and barrels and through into the outhouse.

Hazelrigg reported, "Abiathar and Kyril are round the back, ma'am. Young Denzil can ride to the next farm?"

"He'll never make fifteen miles in this."

Hazelrigg, a stocky, dark man, bundled in a freize coat, pushed the brim of his hat up and spat into the settling snow. "Destructive bastards, soldiers."

She slung the cloak over her right shoulder, leaving left hand and sword-side unencumbered. "The Lord-Architect has the children safe."

She stomped across the yard, boot-heels skidding on the film of white. Warm only by contrast with yesterday's bitter cold, the raw air bit into her. Snow stuck to her eyelashes as she glanced up, looking to see Achitophel's bell-mouthed musket projecting from under the eaves. Cold air seared her bare jaw and ears.

Hooves clattered, muffled on the driveway.

Men on horses loomed through the now-driving snow, huddled in cloaks and hats; the sharp lines of musket barrels jutting up from their silhouettes.

The White Crow narrowed her eyes. Grey bulks emerged against the pale clouds. A horse and rider; another; two more. One. Two. And three more horses, each with two riders tandem on the back.

"Yeah." Cynicism in her tone, that Hazelrigg clearly heard, and a prepared knowledge. "So where's the rest of them . . ."

She brushed her wrist across her eyes, clearing wet flakes. Automatically, despite the absence of belt and blade, she tucked her sword-hand up into the opposite armpit, flexing fingers for warmth and readiness.

"Madam!"

The leading rider attempted to rein in a big dapple mare. The beast dropped her head between her shoulders as soon as the grip on the rein slackened.

Horse-breath huffed, clouding the raw air. The White Crow stepped forward and touched a hand to the horse's foam-rimmed nostrils.

"Are you their captain? You're killing this animal!"

A boot passed within inches of her face as the man swung down from the horse. Snow chalked his felt coat and tricorne hat.

"Madam, I apologise. We gambled with the weather and lost. The beasts suffer as we do."

He took off his hat. Oddly brilliant eyes gazed down from a lined face. Snow settled into the glossy brown curls of his full-bottomed periwig. A man perhaps forty: riding some eighteen stone, and well over six feet tall.

"I have the honour to command this free company of gentlemen-mercenaries." Hat in one hand, the mare's reins in the other, he contrived to sweep a passable low bow.

Her gaze went over his bent back. The other riders sat slumped in the driving cold particles of ice. One gelding whickered.

"Are you the lady of the house, madam?"

Under the coat, faded lace showed at his throat. A scabbarded sword clinked. Snow crusted on scuffed boots. His strong, large-featured face contrasted sharply with the curled wig and lace.

The White Crow stood bareheaded, ignoring the snow soaking through her hair and cold on her scalp. "I'll show you the road to the next estate."

"Madam, earlier this morning I had the honour to give your residence—distantly visible as it was before this con- founded snow—as a rendezvous for the remainder of my company. They will arrive here soon."

"How many is the remainder?"

The big man turned his head, calculating horses and riders present. "Enough, madam."

"We'll send them on after you."

One deep-cuffed hand moved to rest on his hip. He squinted up at the house eaves through the snow. "I'll wager not. You can hardly muster more than ten men, I think; and not so many expert with arms. Madam, it pains me to be impolite. I swear it does. You have food and shelter, my company stand in need, and I have business here."

She met his brightly dangerous eyes, hearing equally com- pounded bluster and humour.

The White Crow lifted her head, looking round at the circle of riders: hard and weary faces visible under the brims of plumed hats. She shook the cloak back from her shoul- ders. Cold cut through her body.

"It isn't as if I haven't stood in your shoes, Captain. But no."

Without shivering, without faltering, she raised her warmed hand and sketched a complex sign on the air.

A rose-and-gold luminescence tinged her fingers, brilliant against the falling snow. Where her hand passed, air coa- lesced and tingled: shone the colour of the absent sun. Ground thrummed underfoot.

Snow like a handful of thrown gravel stung her jaw. The temperature plummetted. Air contracted: blasting icily across the riders, ripping at hats and cloaks, numbing hands. A musket clattered to the cobbles. Men swore.

A watery light emanated from no clear point, unless it was the hands of the White Crow. The little dappled shadows of the snow flocked to her feet. Blue shadows on white snow.

The whiteness rose and flowed about her ankles, warm as fur. She cast the colour of bone and ivory, dipping her hands to skim and touch the wind-devils of snowflakes. Wind-devils that whirled out, hardened, began to become solid . . .

The shapes of great snow leopards prowled across the yard. Blue patterns their pelts, shimmers over muscle and ligament, shadows their great jaws, and sits in their eyes of flowers. The colour of bone is cold in their mouths.

One brown gelding screamed. Its head jerked up and pulled the reins from a dismounted mercenary's hand, and its forefeet rose, hung pawing; and the bugling scream ripped out as it backed, jostled, and half-reared again. The other horses began to back and fret.

The White Crow paused with one hand halfway to her dagger. She drew no confirming blood.

"Madam!"

Still holding the mercenary captain's gaze, his face blue-white in the sudden freeze, she all but completed the air-drawn hieroglyph, then dropped her hand to the dapple mare's neck.

Potential predators faded into greyness. The exhausted horse whickered and raised her head.

Snow ran into water around the White Crow's boots. Yard-cobbbles gleamed. Sudden warmth breathed into their faces.

"*Magia!*" The captain swore.

A horse clattered back. One sword among the group snicked back into its scabbard. She heard startled whispers.

"My name is White Crow. Master-Physician Valentine White Crow, of the Invisible College. Now. If we don't have muskets, I suspect you don't have *magia*. Probably we could discuss this in a civilised manner."

The man's gaze went past her. The White Crow took two steps back before she glanced over her shoulder.

"Excuse me." Three skidding steps took her across the wet stone. She grabbed the Lord-Architect's fat arm as he walked into the yard. "Casaubon! What in damnation do you think you're—"

"*CALMADY!*"

The White Crow fingered her cold ear, a pained expression on her face. " 'Calmady'?"

The Lord-Architect, beaming, lumbered between horses and riders to enfold the mercenary captain in an ursine embrace. "Rot it! Pollexfen Calmady!"

Captain Pollexfen Calmady studied the hole in the heel of his stocking. He eased down in the wing-armed kitchen chair, one boot still on, sinking his chin into the yards of lace swathing his throat. "That's luck. Death and damnation, but it is!"

The heat of the oven fireplace beat against him.

"Post sentries, Captain?"

"Post lookouts for Bevil, death take him." Calmady shut his eyes. The gentlemen-mercenary's footsteps departed.

"Messire Captain."

Without moving anything else, he opened his eyes. Half a dozen mercenaries, in various states of disarray, lounged in the great fireplace. A pale snowlight shone on the kitchen's whitewashed vaults. He smelled salt bacon, herbs, and sawdust.

A redheaded woman of perhaps thirty sat with one hip up on the scrubbed table. She watched him with tawny-red eyes.

"Messire Captain, I want some answers."

"Apply to your husband for them, madam. I confess myself so exhausted, I couldn't plead my case were I before the Lord Chief Justice herself."

"Try."

Slowly, he finished unbuttoning his frieze coat, letting it fall open. Melting snow crusted his scarlet silk breeches and the embroidered hem of his scarlet waistcoat. He sighed.

"Calmady of Calmady," he rumbled. "That is my lord Gadsbury; *that* is Lord Rule; over there you'll find Lady Arbella Lacey, Sir John Hay, Margrave Linebaugh, the Countess of . . . but they have manners enough to introduce themselves."

He saw the woman's mouth tighten.

Lord Rule, black periwig somewhat wetly draggled, swept the plumed hat from his head and made an exquisite bow. "Servant, ma'am."

"Likewise, madam, likewise." Bess, Lady Winslow, flashed paste rings, whirling a lace kerchief in a flourish. She stretched one silk-breeched leg to the fire, hand casually resting over the larger of its patches.

"I don't like gentlemen-mercenaries." The woman's mouth remained tight. "I don't like your particular brand of noble brutality."

"As Physician-magus, madam, you're at liberty to dislike what you please." Pollexfen Calmady watched snow-light glint off the last remaining gold rings on his large fingers. "Were you both scholar and soldier, as some of your College are, we should find a less cold welcome."

"I am—I have been a Scholar-Soldier. As for the present, your welcome depends solely on your conduct in my house."

She slipped from the table to stand on the stone flags, hands cupping elbows, looking at him with her head cocked to one side. He let her hostility slide by him. He leaned forward, smothered in the riding-coat, to pull off his other boot; failed, and snapped fingers for Gadsbury. The stocky man knelt and dug his fingers into leather, mud, and slush.

"Any sign of him, Gadsbury?"

"Not yet, Captain." The boot jerked free.

"Boy's a damn *fool*."

Gadsbury grunted agreement, rising. "Anyone who doesn't make it through this soon isn't going to make it at all."

Cold blasted through the cracks of the kitchen door. A few particles of snow dusted the floor. Calmady rested his foot down, wincing as the stocking-hole let bare skin touch the flagstones. Beyond the snow-pasted glass, a blizzard whirled. The wind's buffets echoed through the kitchens.

"Light the lanterns." The redhaired woman signalled to a clutch of country-dressed men and women whom Calmady assumed to be the servants, and turned back to him. "Messire Captain, you—"

Thunderous bangs rattled the kitchen door.

Lord Rule, having applied his eye to the crack, wiped sleet from his face and wig and unbarred the door. It clanged open. A cluster of figures stumbled in, shedding cloaks, shouting. Calmady sat straighter in the chair. As they saw him, they quietened.

"Captain—"

"Report first—"

"—captain!"

A familiar gangling figure pushed his way forward to the fireplace, swept off his triple-plumed hat, and bowed to Calmady, scattering snow over flagstones and Bess, Lady Winslow, impartially. The woman-mercenary swore. The boy pushed his long yellow curls out of his face.

"Father—*Captain*, I mean—we did it!"

Lieutenant Bevil beamed with a sixteen-year-old's enthusiasm. The tip of his sharp nose shone red in his cold-mottled face, and a drop of moisture hung from it. He fumbled, stripping off lacework gloves from practically unprotected hands. "No trouble! My lord Thompson, be so kind as to show the captain."

Calmady turned his head. The Physician-magus, caught in mid-speech, shut her mouth and leaned up against the inglenook wall in silence. Their cloaks shed, in blue and scarlet and orange silks and brocades the gentlemen-mercenaries crowded close. The boy pulled his torn lace cuffs into more splendid falls. The high folds of his cravat, soaked, subsided onto his azure-silk shoulders.

"Here!" he proclaimed.

Enthusiastically, Thompson and Arbella Lacey spilled the

contents of four hessian sacks onto the kitchen floor. A dozen shirts, two patched doublets, odd pairs of hose, and innumerable sheets piled up. Calmady met the boy's pale blue eyes.

"Bevil . . ."

"You *said* we needed material to patch our uniforms with. We ambushed Captain Sforza's troop. We stole their laundry! It's perfect." Doubt crossed his raw features. "Someone's going to have to wash it first . . ."

Very still, Calmady looked down at the heap of dirty clothes.

"I have a message." Bevil frowned with effort. "From Captain Huizinga. He's holed up on the other side of the moor. He says would we mind returning the cow we stole from them. Their troop doesn't have any milk. He says he'll exchange her for two hens—but one of them isn't a good layer."

Loud argument broke out: Gadsbury staggering to his feet to proclaim the value of the bargain, Hay contradicting; others on their knees, sorting through the clothes-pile. Pollexfen Calmady sat motionless.

"Captain."

He turned his head and met the redheaded woman's gaze. Prepared to challenge at the merest hint of a smile, and (for all his exhaustion) to draw sword on a magus if this particular one should chance to laugh.

With equal parts gravity and courtesy, the woman said, "I came down to bring you a message, messire Captain. The Lord-Architect invites you—all—to dinner."

Desire stares out through the leafless February branches. Snow rapidly penetrates the thick copse.

Cut aside and trampled, barbed-wire coils. Fractured ice feathers down to lay on rusting black spikes. Beyond the forest's edge, noon darkens.

Fast filling up, the second mercenary patrol's tracks turn unmistakably towards the isolated hall.

The snow-front lowers the sky to the horizon. Cold stings her cheeks. Wind lifts the matt-black tendrils of Desire's hair. Her greatcoat billows over belted layers of skirts and doublets.

She carries a heavy dead branch, resting it against her shoulder, a two-handed grip ready to swing it in a crippling blow.

The blizzard drives hard across the heathland beyond the forest. She staggers out, head down, at once ankle-deep in snow. Blasting wind robs her of breath.

Forced on, aware that she follows mercenary tracks, aware that there is only one place to which the tracks can lead; without shelter and without opportunity to reconnoitre, Desire plods towards the unknown hall.

"Well done," the White Crow said softly.

Abiathar rested one hip on the arm of the White Crow's carved wooden chair, wiping her burn-scarred hands on her apron.

"Now if they weren't too exhausted and drink-besotten to realise, they'd see this is food fit only for pigs, which is after all what they are. Still, you call a dinner for fifteen extra at an hour's notice, and half-burned and half-raw is what you'll *get.*"

The White Crow grinned at the older woman.

The tattered silks and faded brocade of the gentlemen-mercenaries gleamed in the snow-light of noon. Lord Rule leaned back, the pale light shining on the rouge on his cheeks. The Margrave Linebaugh fingered a brown beauty-spot. Hands formally gloved, the company made elegant and drunken conversation.

Thick flakes sudded past outside the tall windows. A haze of smoke and the heat of drink and noise made the hall loud.

"They may prove friends of at least one of us . . ." Wincing at the ringing shouts, the White Crow added, "Kitterage where he should be? And Hazelrigg?"

"Both with broadswords and muskets, ma'am."

The White Crow leaned back in her chair, chin down on the lace ruffles of her shirt, the baby cradled in one arm. Around the four dining-tables hastily put together in a hollow square, Pollexfen Calmady and the gentlemen-mercenaries sat drinking. She eyed the Lord-Architect sardonically.

Abiathar shrugged. "My cousin had soldiers billetted on the farm. Et the place bare. When they wasn't out stripping and robbing some honest man for the fun of it, that is. Roughneck rogues and drunkards. Of whatever quality."

Watching her go, the White Crow shifted the shawl-wrapped baby to her other elbow, careful of the leather doublet's studs. Missing the weight of a swept-hilted rapier jabbing her hip.

"You're not very *fashionable* in the country, ma'am, are you? I see you don't even *paint* for dinner."

The White Crow raised her head. The boy Bevil Calmady, in what she at first took to be watered (and instantly concluded was only water-*stained*) blue tabby-silk doublet and breeches, stood by the empty chair at her left.

She said, "This isn't dinner, it's midday; and not by my choice."

A spray of plumes buckled to his hatband fell forward, brushing his rouged cheeks. He fingered a beauty-spot which, like four others, had been pasted over a cluster of acne.

She searched her slashed doublet sleeves with one hand and held up a small linen square. "True, we're very unfashionable. Have a kerchief. Your lipstick's smudged."

The boy, midway through adjusting this, snapped his fob-mirror shut, suddenly distracted.

"You have a baby!"

He hooked a chair up with his heel and sat down, ignoring the growing revelry—drunkenness and relief from cold in about equal measures—of the other gentlemen-mercenaries.

His pale blue eyes gleamed. He leaned forward, proffering a finger. Under the table, the White Crow's free hand loosened the dagger in her boot.

A hand no larger than a half-crown shut around the boy's finger. The orange-haired baby opened unfocussed eyes of a shocking blue and dispiritedly announced, "Yawp!"

Bevil's face glowed. He rested his arm on the chair so that the child's grip on his forefinger was unstrained. "It likes me!"

"*Yawp!*"

"It's a she." Calculating uses of trust, the White Crow added, "Would you like to hold her?"

"*Could* I?"

Oblivious to implications or danger, the boy shook back lace falls at his wrist, and carefully cradled the baby against his shoulder. It vented a resonant burp. The White Crow stood, walking past the backs of chairs—fifteen or so men and women, in their thirties mostly, worn hard with long campaigning—and around the room.

"Your baby, ma'am?" Pollexfen Calmady called, raising a pewter mug.

"My daughter Jadis." She nodded to the solemn eight-year-old, on his chair beside the Lord-Architect. "And my son, Jared."

" 'Jared,' " Pollexfen Calmady said gravely, "which in the Hebrew tongue is *rose*. I salute you, young man, as the emblem of your true Queen."

Jared's small, stolid face froze. One serving-man banged a plate down in front of Lord Gadsbury. The White Crow winced at sudden tension. Apparently unaware of it—his gaze skidding across the servants as if they were human furniture—Calmady raised his mug again. He stood, elegantly massive in long curled wig and beauty-spots.

"I'll wager nobody present will fail me in this. The toast is, *the Queen and her Hangman!*"

Before the White Crow could speak, Abiathar shouted

from the serving hatch: "No one ever drank that toast in Roseveare. No one ever will. I'll give you a toast that isn't to that oyster-whore Queen Carola! The toast is, *the Lights and Perfections.*"

"No toasts." White Crow took Pollexfen Calmady's mug and set it down on the linen cloth. She leaned against the table, on the far side of him from the Lord-Architect. "Captain, you say you have business here?"

He shook his head, laughing, the curls of the periwig flying. "Irony, madam. *Video meliora proboque, deteriora sequor*: I see the better way and approve it, but I follow the worse way. I drink still to her most Royal Majesty Carola—but, being gentleman-mercenary and commanded by pay, I bring the Protectorate's commission."

With some satisfaction the White Crow leaned back against the edge of the table, weight on her wrists, and crossed her booted ankles. "Now, see you, it was only a matter of time! I came home expecting trouble."

"Madam—"

"It was only a matter of which faction got here first. This family's always had influence, and wealth, and I have knowledge of *magia: Someone* had to want to use that."

Pollexfen Calmady put his hands on the chair-arms, buttoned-back cuffs and lace falling to hide his fists. "Truthfully, madam, my commission isn't to you."

"I—what?"

"Here's my man!" Pollexfen Calmady slapped his embroidered gauntlet across the Lord-Architect's shoulder. Casaubon took his nose out of a beer-mug, spilling brown liquid down his ruffled shirt, and looked up with an unassailably guileless amazement.

"Me?" He chuckled resonantly, caught the White Crow's eye, and stopped short.

The gentleman-mercenary continued with distaste. "The damned bitch-General herself wants an architect. I go where I'm hired. Consequently, I'm hired to escort you to the

Prince of Peace and Architecture, the most sovereign Protector of this realm—and I wish you joy of her—the great General Olivia."

White Crow, slightly pink about the ears, looked back at Casaubon in time to see him steeple his fingers and remark: "Ah! They must be having problems building the eye of the sun."

Pollexfen Calmady turned and spat over his shoulder into the open fire. "Without the blood royal, a pox-rotten mess they make of it! I saw the old bitch-General Olivia herself up on the foundation stones, chrism and sacrifice, *did* it work? No! Did she get away with a whole skin? *Just* barely. Plague take her!"

"Still," he added, with some satisfaction, "the temple's no further up than the lower walls, and not like to be, if tavern-rumour's true. What's built up by day is undermined by night, and they've taken to finding dead workmen there, too."

"Murdered?" the White Crow guessed.

"No. Murder, madam, would be a matter for the Watch. *She* wants an architect."

The door scraped open.

Plates scattered, swords ripped from sheaths. Abiathar, at the back of Bevil Calmady's chair, suddenly rested a sharp skewer in the hollow of the boy's ear, trapping him motionless with the baby in his arms. His startled gaze flicked to the double doors.

Edward Kitterage stumbled through, musket falling from under one long arm, his flaxen hair plastered across his face. On one arm and hip he lugged the unconscious body of a young woman. Snow crusted her sopping black hair. What skin showed under her bundled clothes was mottled blue and purple with cold.

The massive bulk of the Lord-Architect surged up, chair clattering over.

"Soup," the fat man shouted. "Hot wine! Abiathar! Quickly, woman!"

He caught and cradled the unconscious woman in his arms, resting her across the vast expanse of his chest and belly.

"Doing a round," Kitterage grunted, wary gaze on the gentlemen-mercenaries. "Found her out by the yard-entrance. Fell over her. She dead?"

"Not quite." The White Crow touched fingers to the young woman's throat, skin chilled over invisible veins. A faint pulse of rose light remained where the White Crow touched, shaped in the whorls of a fingerprint.

With the swiftness of practise, she withdrew the bee-pin from her braids, pricked her index finger, and smearily traced a hierogylph across the young woman's brow. She smoothed back wet black hair.

Long lashes lay on clear-skinned cheeks, dotted with melting snow. Tears oozed from under one lid. Sharply delicate earlobes and nostrils were translucent white. She fingered the full lower lip down. A shiver of warm breath touched her skin.

"What has the same Signatures . . . ?" The White Crow mused aloud. "Fireweed and gorse-flower, for the essence of the Sun and warmth. Mandragora and moon-root for sleep. Blood for blood. Kitterage, I'll want you to make liver-broth. Put her . . ."

Her forehead wrinkled in concentration.

"Full moon, the Water-Carrier dominant, what ascendant . . . put her in the West High Chamber; I'll come to her there."

The Lord-Architect wheeled and walked towards the stairs, carrying the tall young woman without effort. The White Crow stared after him.

"She's *stunning.*"

Spoken to the air, her words found an ear not far off. Pollexfen Calmady guffawed. "Madam, you're jealous!"

An odd smile crossed her face.

"Not precisely," the White Crow said.

II

Pollexfen Calmady put down a card. *"Ten of Lances . . .* What ails your lady?"

"Knight of Grails. My trick. At the parting of roads that all Scholar-Soldiers come to. She has studied and become a healer," the Lord-Architect Casaubon said, "a Master-Physician. And she misses the blade, and hates herself."

Pollexfen Calmady upended a pewter mug of beer and wiped his lips with a lace kerchief. He dealt again. "All I can say, sir, is that your letter painted her in damned pastel colours!"

Casaubon said hastily, "I didn't write to you."

"So you didn't. I was forgetting." He belched.

Icy wind screamed. Tall windows creaked open. Bess, Lady Winslow, standing by one, callused hands on the frame, kicked glass panels out so that the driving snow blew in. She leaned back to shout to Lord Rule, who tossed her another wine bottle.

Outside, the lords Thompson and Gadsbury pissed steaming yellow jets onto the terrace in competition, perilously close to Hay who, having wrestled Arbella Lacey to the flagstones, was putting snow down the tall woman's bodice and getting an ill-aimed knee between the legs for his trouble.

"*Dabit deus his quoque finem.*" Pollexfen Calmady rubbed the heel of his hand into his eye-socket. "God will grant me an end even to *these* troubles!"

Bevis sat with one knee up in a chair, a cittern across his lap, picking out melancholy tunes. "They're a fine troop, Father."

"A fine troop of the destitute, I grant you!"

Cold yellow, the sky wept flakes that moved with the aerodynamics of feathers. Snow built up on terrace, balustrade, statues, and lawns. Eight inches and rising. Cold gales seared in the open window.

"*Close that!* Apologies." Pollexfen Calmady kicked at the snow on the rug, sprawling in the chair before the roaring fire, thumbing through his cards.

The Lord-Architect's fat fingers prodded his cards with delicate concentration. He reached deep into the pocket of his sprigged velvet frock-coat, unearthed two rose-nobles, and wiped them on his sleeve. A trail of grease scummed the satin.

"I perceive," he rumbled, "that you still play for stakes vastly too high for your pocket."

"I do. Let me see." Pollexfen Calmady reached across, gripped the Lord-Architect's wrist, and turned it over. A small white scar crossed the flesh, an inch above the wrist's creases of flesh. "Not gone yet, then? Blood brother still."

Four o'clock light glinted in the mercenary captain's eyes. It silvered the waterfall-curls of his periwig, gleamed from brocade sleeves and breast and breeches. Something of the unnatural brilliant dark of daytime snow found an echo in those eyes.

"Madam White Crow." He loosed Casaubon's wrist as the woman entered the long room.

"Our visitor's sleeping. Well, say you, are you persuaded to town yet?" She rested her arms along the Lord-Architect's shoulders, looking down over his stained satin lapels to his cards. "It smells of collusion to me, I must say."

"My *little* one . . ."

Pollexfen Calmady broke out in a great laugh. He threw his hand of cards down and grabbed the jug to refill his mug. "There's for you, boy! The worst folly of a man is thinking he can *conceal* his folly. Do you confess to her now. The odds are in your favour, if I'm a judge."

The Lord-Architect Casaubon spread fat-fingered hands, glancing over his cushioned shoulder at the redhaired woman. A slight pink coloured his earlobes. "Well . . ."

The woman stepped back. Her thumb hooked over her breeches-belt. For some moments she stared at Pollexfen Calmady. "This Protector of yours—"

"Not mine!"

"—must have architects of her own."

"A few poor renegade-architects, perhaps. Geometry being considered in that court a Black Art." Pollexfen Calmady snorted. "Listen to me. 'Renegade.' "

An odd smile moved her mouth. He caught some quirk of humour that vanished before he could identify it. She said, "Renegades have their own honour."

"Madam, at a very respectable price."

"Hmm. I suspect I would have known, even if you hadn't told me, that you were an old friend of his." She wound a coil of the Lord-Architect's copper-red hair around her forefinger, tugging it sharply. "How long since Casaubon last dragged you into this sort of foolery?"

The Lord-Architect said hollowly, "*He* inveigles *me*. Always has. All through university."

"I remember the first day of your arrival at the Sun of Science." Pollexfen Calmady regarded the fan of cards in his large fingers. "Thin as a lath, in a filthy black doublet, on fire to show how much you knew of the Craft, and how much better than anyone else you could be at it."

The Lord-Architect fetched up a belch from the recesses of his stomach.

"I *did* do it better. Pox rot you, I still do!"

"But not in the city you were born to?"

"I am allowing them to try the experiment of republicanism," Casaubon said loftily. "They'll come crawling back to me, any day now."

"Ha!" the White Crow said.

"But you were right," Pollexfen Calmady concluded softly, looking at his five-guinea hand. "I did indeed gamble away my inheritance—estate, house, shares, and all."

" 'Thin as a lath,' " the White Crow echoed.

"We were younger then." The gentleman-mercenary discarded the *Six of Grails*. "And of more general service to the world, I doubt not; but forgive me, madam, would you have him any other way?"

"If pressed to an answer . . . no, I would not."

The Lord-Architect pulled her onto his lap in an exuberant hug, played the *Seven of Swords*, and raised an eyebrow at her groan. "Strategy. Forward planning!"

"My trick," Pollexfen Calmady observed.

And night slides in across the curve of the world.

She sprawled across the workbench, asleep.

Air and darkness sang, struck. A warning of *magia* burned under her skin. Her arteries ran with sudden fire.

Hard metal bruised her hand: dagger ripped from its boot-sheath before she stood properly awake. Shaking her head to clear it, the White Crow staggered along the corridor from the herb-room.

The stairs and far hall shouted with drunken rout. A woman screeched a song. Dagger blades screeled, peeling strips from the panelling. One man hacked his heel to the beat of the song. Another—Lord Gadsbury?—vomited as she passed.

She took the narrow wooden steps two at a time. The wall banged her shoulder. Twisting the handle, she wrenched at the nursery door.

Locked. Pain in her wrist jarred her awake. She fumbled the key-chain from under her shirt and opened the door, eyes darting up and down the corridor.

Dim lamplight glared from the muzzle of a musket. The dark man, Hazelrigg, loosened his finger on the trigger at the sight of her. Beyond him, small bed and bassinet stood peacefully occupied.

"Madam?"

"*Whoreson stupid*—not you!" She hit her head with her hand, aghast; threw the key at him, and shouted, "Don't open this door to anyone!" as she spun round and sprinted back down the corridor.

Magia wards fired her blood. Boot-heels hit stairs two at a time; she grabbed at her belt and again missed the presence of a sword.

Footsteps clattered up the stairs behind her.

Third floor: West High Chamber.

The door stood open.

Linen and blankets tumbled down onto the floorboards. A man's back hid half the bed. Thrown back in pillows, mouth loosely open, the young woman's head bounced up and down with the movement of the mattress.

Wig tipped sideways, showing his shaved head, and his breeches tangled around his calves, Pollexfen Calmady sprawled across the bed and the woman. His bare buttocks pumped. Pox-scarred skin shone yellow as old grease in the lamplight. One pale foot jutted from under the man's arm, trapped. Thrown wide, the young woman's other leg jounced and flopped.

Three floors below a fiddle pumped in gruesome counterpoint.

"*Leave her*—"

The bed's uneven leg knocked rhythmically against the floorboards; the man grunting deep in his throat, oblivious.

He dug hard fingers into her left breast, her flesh swelling out pale under his kneading hand, and his nails raked red lines from her nipple to her ribs. The curled wig slipped: his mouth coming down hard on her right breast, chewing, biting; he worried at it, scarlet-faced; lifted a mouth dripping saliva and plunged it down upon hers, thrusting his tongue into her slack mouth. His hips jerked back: slammed forward, the back of her skull hitting the headboard.

The White Crow reversed her grip on the dagger to strike with the hilt; called up *magia* invocations from her sleep-sodden mind:

"*Tagla-mathon-* —"

"Father!"

Something hit her elbow and knocked her against the door-jamb. She glimpsed Bevil Calmady, eyes and mouth gaping. She pushed him aside. He skidded: another body barrelled past both of them. A whiff of familiar smells cut off her automatic reflex: she clamped her mouth shut on a *magia*-word.

"*Calmady!*" The Lord-Architect, flushed and his coat discarded, roared. His footsteps shook the floor. In two strides he crossed the room, grabbed Pollexfen Calmady by the collar of his coat and the back of his knee, digging fingers into muscle. He heaved, twisting: the man screaming at the awkward angle of withdrawal. Casaubon lifted the man bodily up from the bed and threw him. Eighteen stone of bone and muscle smashed a chair and hit the floor.

"*What*—"

Pollexfen Calmady screeched. He reared to his feet, grabbed the bed-hangings, slipped; and stumbled up again. His face burned purple, his eyes ran with water. Vomit stained the front of his brocade coat. He coughed a breath that stank of old wine and half-fermented beer.

"Wha's?— 'S outrageous! 'S damnable! Gut me, I'll rip you!"

"Rapist!"

He slipped again, grabbing a bedpost. The curled wig slid down over his shoulders and fell to the floor. Thick stubble covered his shaven head, brilliant with drops of sweat.

"I did not—"

His shining eyes gained focus. One hand brushed at his ruffles. Tan breeches hobbled his ankles. His engorged penis rocked as he moved.

"She's willing, damn you! Never said a word. Never a protest, my life on it!"

The White Crow slammed her dagger down on the dresser and knelt up on the bed, straightening the young woman's body. Hands on the bloodied thighs, she glared up at Calmady.

"She's *drugged*, you whoreson bastard!"

The man's mouth opened. He stared.

"Yes, you pig-drunk shit! She's sick, she's drugged to make her sleep, to make her well! *How could you—*"

Bending to pull at his breeches, the man fell forward. He hit the floor face-down. The Lord-Architect drew back his foot and kicked Pollexfen Calmady over onto his back, the force of it lifting and throwing his rangy body a yard or more.

Abiathar blocked the door. She pushed the stunned Bevil aside, her head turned back, issuing orders to other servants to keep the gentlemen-mercenaries in the main hall. She gasped, seeing Pollexfen Calmady. "Blind drunk. As like to be fucking our old pig, or whatever he stumbled across, I reckon."

"Drunk? Him? He's too capable of the act to be drunk!" Outrage made the White Crow breathless. "*Bastard!*"

Song echoed harshly up the hall and the corridor. The White Crow smoothed hair back from the young woman's unconscious face. "I'll have to examine her. See what damage . . . Get that boy out of here!"

"I'll take him." The Lord-Architect belched gently.

"Where the fuck were you?" she demanded.

"Dealing with fifteen others in a similar condition." Sharp, if not sober, Casaubon's gaze took in the slumped man, the pale young woman, and the White Crow. "You?"

"I went to the nursery first. I got here too late. I should have been here!"

He reached to put a comforting hand on her shoulder, but the White Crow sat down on the sick-bed, already bending over the sheet-covered form of the younger woman.

*   *   *

The sky is clear all the rest of the night, starshine on the new snow.

Towards morning, laden clouds gather.

"I remember nothing."

The young woman put her hands down between her thighs, under the sheets. Pain stabbed at her face, muscles around her eyes contracting. Swollen flesh half-closed one eye; her lower lip puffy; and yellow bruises, just beginning to come out, marked all one side of her jaw, neck, collar-bone, and breast. She shifted to one buttock, to the other; and leaned back awkwardly against the sloping pillows.

"But reason tells me, had you not drugged my sleep, I could have defended myself."

"You're bruised. Something torn. Don't wipe off what you find down there," the White Crow said, "it's a salve I spent the early hours of this morning making. It should help."

"Should it?"

The White Crow sat down on the edge of the bed. She took cold, slender hands in her own. "Shock—"

"Was he diseased, this man?" Calm dark eyes fixed her. "Am I carrying a child?"

"It'll be some days before I can perform the *magia* to know either. I can do that."

The young woman took both hands back to smooth the hair away from her marked face. "Yes. You're a Master-Physician, of the Invisible College. Valentine called White Crow, of Roseveare."

Dark red brows indented. The White Crow stood. She folded her arms, hands cupping elbows. "You—who are you?"

"My name is Desire-of-the-Lord Guillaime."

"*Ah.*"

The black-haired young woman in the bed regarded her with self-possession. "Are we secret?"

"Reasonably. Do I want," the White Crow mused, "to

hear anything that has to be told to me in secrecy? No, I think I do not. I live a quiet, retired life here in the country. I'll hear nothing that disturbs it."

Desire's black eyes moved under long lashes. The faintest slurring marked her speech, and her tongue licked out to probe her swollen lip. "Not even a plan to fund the escape of Carola?"

White Crow blinked.

"This *is* Carola the Second? Her most Catholic Majesty? Her most indolent Majesty," she added, and then shook her head in annoyance. "I haven't seen the woman since I was twelve. And in any case, Desire-of-the-Lord, you don't have a name that I'd expect to find in the royal court."

The younger woman leaned back, smoothing blankets down around her torso. Linen defined the shape of breasts and stomach. She gritted her teeth and grunted.

"No. I'm a good Protectorate woman, madam."

"That I guessed."

"And to be most honest, no one more wishes the escape of *Regina* Carola than the Protector. Her most Catholic Majesty is a liability. We'd sooner see her in exile."

The White Crow stood. She rested both hands against the carved bedframe, and then took several paces one way, several paces back. The air chilled her skin. Snow-light shone up from the ground and in at the window, bleaching the plastered ceiling.

"This is the trouble, you see. Coming back after so long, belonging to no faction or party, being seen as—" She smiled, curiously, "—new blood. New fodder for the war."

"This house has always stood for the Protectorate."

"This house," the White Crow emphasised, "hasn't seen me since I was thirteen. We had *no* business coming back here; I knew what I was doing when I ran away to join the Scholar-Soldiers; I should never have *consented* to inherit!— It's my inheritance. It isn't my concern."

Desire shaded her eyes with her hand. She moved down

in the bed, painfully and awkwardly pulling sheets and rumpled blankets up about her shoulders.

"But you will do it."

The White Crow turned. The unbruised curve of Desire's shoulders showed smooth, pale, marked with old scars of duty and church discipline. Knotted matt-black hair cushioned the young woman's head.

She reached down to pick at snarls in that soft, sweat-matted hair, flicking a glance at Desire's face.

"Will I?"

"Yes." Black lashes swept down; back. "Because I ask you. Because of what happened to me here."

"That isn't something you use for blackmail!"

The White Crow's hand, still moving among the tangles of hair, felt hot moisture on the young woman's cheek. She stopped as if her muscles had locked.

"The Protector wants Valentine Roseveare."

"Yes."

The room's air is chill, snow-bright; the kind of morning in which to scrunch down under heavy blankets, in cloth-scented warmth and safety.

The White Crow said, "I suppose I had better come to London."

III

Bevil Calmady's breath whitened the morning air. The young man put his heels into the big gelding's sides and maneuvered down the snow-covered slope. The coach-and-six rattled down, scant yards away, its brakes squealing.

"*Hei!*"

He spurred past Gadsbury and Lacey without looking at them, coming up with the coach as the slope levelled out. Hooves threw up clots of snow and half-frozen mud.

The snow-covered heath and moorland stretched away, frighteningly clear under a pale blue sky. Against that sky the distant white hills shone; all their shadows blue and lilac. Leafless shrubs pricked the air. Bevil swallowed, cold drying his throat.

"Mistress Abiathar!" He leaned over, peering through the coach's horn-shutters.

The nurse huddled in blankets and a massive coat, the orange-haired baby almost smothered in its swaddling. Jared sat as stiff-backed as is possible for an eight-year-old in a jolting coach.

On the far seat, the black-haired young woman lay asleep. One heeled, black boot peeped out from under her six or seven layers of skirts. A thin coil of hair pasted to her cheek.

Abiathar's voice carried over the rattle of coach wheels, springs, team-harness, and the driver's cries. "Let her sleep if she can. Don't you be bothering her."

"I won't. I wouldn't."

"I don't say *like father like son*, mark."

His cheeks heated. Abruptly spurring the gelding, pulling its head round, he galloped away up the track. Almost a quarter-mile separated first and second coaches now, Abiathar's weighed down by the luggage and one mercenary guard on the roof.

Bess, Lady Winslow, pulled her mare aside as he passed. Her gloved hand went up as if she would have flourished her plumed hat in usual flamboyance. She arrested the gesture and rubbed awkwardly at her mouth. Cold stung tears, leaking from the corners of Bevil's eyes.

Strung out along the moorland road, point and guard, nearly twenty riders paced the coaches. The bright dots of satin and brocade startled the morning, scarlet and viridian against the muted browns of snow-pasted shrubs and low wooden fences.

"Be well enough if we reach London by Tuesday."

Startled by a close voice, he rubbed the back of his gloved hand across his face and turned in the saddle.

The Master-Physician White Crow rode straight-backed, draped in a heavy leather cloak. She raised one hand to push her ermine-lined hood back from her face, and loosen the neck-clasp.

"Madam." Bevil stood in the saddle and bowed. Chill air cut through the worn places in his silver-embroidered blue silk breeches. "You think the snow will hold off until then?"

"Trust me."

He stared uncomprehendingly, hearing an acidity in her voice and not knowing why. She shook the grey horse's reins, moving to pace him, to one side of the snow thrown up by the lead coach.

"You're wise not to choose to be rattled about inside one of those." He looked up shyly from under fair lashes, frantic to steer the conversation. "You must be more comfortable riding—"

"I am *not*. You try riding a horse in this condition, why don't you?"

Bevil Calmady hesitated, bemused by what he was not entirely certain was a rhetorical question.

The White Crow added, "You don't happen to have a couple of kerchiefs I could borrow?"

Bevil hooked the reins over the saddle-horn and searched his pockets, finally extracting two darned silk kerchiefs. He passed them to her, watching as she tucked them down the front of her doublet.

"What are you doing?"

She took her hand out of her shirt and unkinked her elbow. "Leaking, if it's any of your damn business!"

"Oh." Face bright red, Bevil busied himself with the gelding's reins. The big horse skittered, one hoof skidding on a patch of ice. He recovered, spurring ahead.

"*Boy!*"

He found himself level with the lead coach's window. Inside, Pollexfen Calmady looked up from where he and the Lord-Architect Casaubon sat either side of a let-down card-table dealing *One-and-Twenty*, slammed the window-frame down, and leaned his head out.

"Is the bitch dead, or like to die? No? No! Then stop giving me those whey-faced looks!"

Confusion and anger choked Bevil's voice. He shook his head rapidly, fair hair flying.

"Well, damn you, then! For a puppy who won't own his own father!"

"*Who would?*" His voice broke, squeaked into childish registers.

"Can't a man make a plain *mistake*? And what is she but some cast-off camp whore of Huizinga's or Sforza's? Gods! Sanctimonious boys—"

"We've missed the road, I think." The White Crow's voice cut across the shouting. Bevil leaned forward in the saddle, seeing her ride at the coach's opposite window and snap her fingers for the Lord-Architect's attention.

The fat man, bundled to the chins in a fur-trimmed red velvet morning-robe, leaned his elbow on the window-frame and stared where she pointed. His copper-gold hair, scraped back and tied with a string of black velvet, shone with grease, and the swell of the robe over his belly was stained with old vestiges of egg and soup. He sniffed.

"You may be right, little one. Pull over ahead there, and I'll discover."

Blind with a thundering pulse, Bevil Calmady rode ahead.

The sun, low in the winter sky, touched stonework with a paleness that hardly deserved to be called warmth. Cold air froze his wet eyelashes. He blinked. The burnt-out shell of a moorland church stood in a hollow, snow whitening walls and rubble. Shattered glass lined one pointed window. The weathercock still stood on the half-demolished spire.

He let the gelding pick a way down towards it, reins resting. The animal's body warmed his booted legs. The Lord-Architect plodded down through the ankle-deep snow, voluminous robe flying and padded arms waving for balance. "Boy—"

Bevil Calmady gritted his teeth. "Sir."

One fat, gloved hand beckoned. He nudged the mount the few paces. The fat man's head was on a level with his knee, his breath clouding the air. It took Bevil a second to realise that the object held up to him was a metal flask.

"Try it, my boy. You look as though you need it."

Abruptly, he grabbed the flask and took a deep swallow. A honey taste stayed on his lips. "Th—"

Tears leaked out of his eyes; he coughed, muffled it, coughed again, and finally wheezed air into his lungs and seared throat.

"—thank you. Sir. What *is* that?"

"A recipe of my own," the big man said smugly. He lifted

his face. Cold blotched his cheeks and chin. Startlingly acute
blue eyes fixed on Bevil. "No reason why you shouldn't ride
in the other coach. Abiathar always complains she could use
help with the baby, and my little one there is thinking of
other things now."

Bevil followed his gaze to the White Crow. The woman
sat her horse still, staring at the snow-covered hills. She
stripped the glove from one hand and held up her fingers
for the feel of the air to inform her.

"Will she trust me with the baby?"

"She did last night."

"That was before." The gelding nosed fruitlessly at snow-
covered heather. "Sir, if I hadn't seen it . . . It's a tavern
or whorehouse joke, isn't it? A wench raped sleeping or
unwilling. If I hadn't *seen* it. Oh god, how could he!"

Lithely, he kicked feet free of the stirrups and slid to the
ground. The earth hit the soles of his boots, no give in it,
and he staggered, for the first time aware that this is the
winter ground that breaks bones.

"He's my *father*! I'm ashamed."

The Lord-Architect Casaubon said nothing. He placed one
heavy arm, with immense gentleness, around Bevil Calmady's shoulders. After a moment, Bevil nodded.

"Tell me, sir, how do you hope to find direction from
this?"

A spatter of musket-fire rang out.

Mounted, spurring, all ingrained instinct; the gelding wal-
lowing knee-deep in an unsuspected hollow. The top of the
rise came on him before he realised. Bevil reined in, sword
drawn. Far, far back—sounds carry over snow—puffs of
flame briefly showed. Too far to smell the powder. A cluster
of riders. He narrowed his eyes. One scout in saffron brocade waved a feathered hat: signalling *few and driven off.*

Beside the coach, where the team of six horses stamped
and breathed plumes of white air, Captain Pollexfen Calmady raised his sword and brandished it once. A rider began

to canter back from point. He looked up at the still-mounted Master-Physician.

"Yes, madam. Chessboard wars, as you say, between gentlemen-mercenaries. But do you prefer the reign of footpads and highway robbers or the conditions of civil war? I'd wager that you don't. *Ubi solitudinem faciunt pacem appellant*: they create a desolation and call it peace."

The redhaired woman made no answer. She turned her head, looking past Bevil to the Lord-Architect, where he stood by the ruined church.

"Well? Are we in our way, or out of it?"

Bevil Calmady looked at the sun-yellowed stone. The Lord-Architect stood before the walls, arms crossed, the folds of his red velvet robe wet and white with snow. He sniffed, and with a sideways motion of the head wiped his nose on the black fur collar. A silver trail smeared. Casaubon straightened his massive shoulders and called up to the weathercock:

"Which way to London-town?"

Metal shrieked. The hammered brass eagle swung on its broken pole, creaking to face down the lefthand fork of the track. The bas-relief beak flashed back sunlight. It cried:

"*East and south! Mark me, mark me! East and south from here!*"

That day and night the skies remain cloudless, free of snow.

Two days' dirt engrained the whorls of her fingers.

The White Crow sat against a half-demolished brick wall, arms on knees, blinking at her snow-washed hands. The bonfire's blast seared at her face. Dawn froze her back. Above, a sky clear as water and early as sin birthed light.

"Sleep?"

She glanced over at Lady Arbella Lacey. The woman's nose showed in midst of rolled blankets and cloak, nothing

else visible. The White Crow grinned. "About an hour before midnight. Too cold after. You?"

"Madam, not a wink."

An anonymous voice from another roll of blankets observed, "Then you stay awake damn noisily, and snore while
you do it!"

The White Crow rubbed her hands against her frozen
cheeks.

The quietness and expanded senses that come with outdoor sleeping enveloped her, and all campaign reflexes—the
ability to wait, and wait again, without impatience; to talk;
to draw on inner resources; to think nothing, only to act—
all filled her with a familiar ease. She stared through bitter
air at the coach, the fire, the hobbled horses.

"—and then they both stopped in the hallway, in front of
a suit of *armour*."

The black-haired Lord Rule's voice rose. He gestured,
one hand in its embroidered gauntlet pinning down Lord
Gadsbury, where they both stood stamping their feet on the
other side of the fire.

"Too drunk to know their own names, both of them, and
Bess looked up at this thing, all six foot of it, full plate
armour and helm, and *she* said—"

"—'I want to hear it talk before I fight it!' " the short man
completed, grinning. "Man, *they* were drunk? I was standing right next to you when that happened, and you too rat-
ted to know it."

"I admit I may have been a little inconvenienced."

Rule adjusted his cocked hat, caught the White Crow's
eye, and removed his hat again to bow, making much play
with the plume.

"Madam: good morning."

"Morning." She nodded to both: Gadsbury a head shorter
than the younger man; both in mud-marked lace and satin,
wrapped around with thick woollen cloaks. An effort shifted
her from the wall. Movement chilled her: she rubbed at her
arms and stood.

Now the burnt-out cottage showed as little more than a floor plan: a few walls no more than waist-high, acting as shelter for the slumped forms of sleeping gentlemen-mercenaries and horses. Numb with cold, her feet knocking against broken bricks, she went aside to relieve herself. Empty moorland stretched away under haze and snow.

"Rule's ridiculous." The tall redhead, Bess, fell into step beside her as they finished, and walked back through the deserted and burned herb-garden, lacing up her doublet. "This is the man, mark you, I once heard in the thick of an artillery barrage, telling young Bevil he should please not sweat, since he'd be spoiling a five-hundred-pound suit of clothes!"

The White Crow chuckled. Aches shifted in her shoulders and back, shaken loose by walking. Anticipating later sleep in the coach, when the sun should be high and the day as warm as winter might make it, she wrapped her hands about her arms and nodded towards the fire, where the Marquis of Linebaugh and Bevil Calmady now stood.

"The hell with that: can he make coffee?"

Bess, Lady Winslow, looked down her prominent, frost-reddened nose at Lord Rule, where he squatted over a boiling can at the fire. "Indifferent bad coffee, madam, and distinctly worse tea; but what would you? He was hardly born to this."

Bevil Calmady tipped a shot of brandy into his tea mug and clinked it against Gadsbury's. "The Queen and her Hangman."

"Listen to the boy, will you? He thinks he's a soldier." Gadsbury appealed to the cold morning. Arbella Lacey, rumpled and newly risen, chuckled. Gadsbury stabbed a blunt finger at her. "You're no better. I remember *you* in your first battle—'Oh, sergeant, they're shooting at us!' "

The woman grinned. "Yes, and what did you say? 'That's all right, girl, they're the enemy. They're allowed!' "

"When I was a Scholar-Soldier—"

Light flashed. The White Crow broke off.

The green-painted coach stood with its window-curtains drawn, no sign of the Lord-Architect or Abiathar waking. Light flashed again beyond it. She walked rapidly across the frosted, exposed cottage floor, sliding into automatic concealment behind the coach. Her dirt-grained fingers' reached to her empty belt.

Hobbled, the older of the coach-horses stood mouthing in its feedbag. Jared sat astride, bareback, short legs jutting out horizontally. His small shoulders taut, and both coldreddened hands clenched about the hilt, he held up a curved hanger.

The blade flashed pale light, wobbling, weighty.

"You cut thus, forward and down . . ." Pollexfen Calmady reached up, pointing. Dried mud marked the green woollen cloak about his broad shoulders, staining his curled periwig and the braid on his plumed hat. One gauntleted hand moved, mirroring the small boy's tentative lowering of the blade.

"Here." He reached up and took the sword: a large man, bulky, ponderous. Her breath came short, anticipating the sudden metamorphosis; always there, always shocking: movement from the shoulder and so *quick*—wrist, arm, shoulder in sudden motion; coordination too swift to be recognised. The metal whipped in figure-eight arcs, bright against the dawn.

"Always paying attention to the main purpose of a cavalry stroke, which is," he observed, "not to cut off your horse's ears."

Over Jared's surprised laugh, he added, "Madam, good morning. I find talent but no enthusiasm here; still, *altissima quaeque flumina minimo sono labi*: the deepest rivers flow with the least sound."

His voice blotted the others out.

"You—" Sudden cold bit her gut; forty-eight hours camaraderie vanishing with the return of memory. Shame tanged, a revulsion against speaking to the gentlemen-mercenaries, as if that could prove some collaboration in her. The White Crow walked towards the coach-horse, scenting old sweat and new perfume on Calmady's clothes. Reflexes kept her a step outside his immediate range.

He slotted hanger into scabbard with a click that echoed across the morning, and stood with gauntleted hands on hips. "Do you think I'd harm a boy, and myself with my own son here?"

"Jarrie, tell Abiathar I'm on my way to feed your sister."

"Yes, mama." Swivelling his legs around with difficulty, the boy slid, dropped four feet to the ground, and walked towards the closed coach, tugging doggedly at his long coat to straighten it.

The morning quiet broke with noises. Voices called across the snowy, deserted landscape. One man coughed. Horse-tack clinked, being lifted onto mounts; Arbella Lacey hacked and spat. Meat sizzled on the fire and the smell filled the White Crow's mouth with saliva.

Impossible, now, to walk back to the companionable fire.

"Stay out of my sight. If you can't do that, don't speak. *Stay clear of me.*"

Urbane, the big man drew off one embroidered gauntlet, and wiped his mouth with the lace at his cuff. "I apologise if you find your husband somewhat surly this morning. Throughout our long acquaintance it's been his desire to outdrink me; last night, as on many another occasion, I fear that he failed. My condolences."

"How he can drink with you—"

"Madam, I've known him long and long."

"He never spoke of you."

"No . . ."

The light of very early morning, pale as water, found a reflection in Calmady's eyes. His lined face creased against brightness. The White Crow shivered, feeling every snow-covered wall, every frost-cracked tile of this burned-out and exposed kitchen, every mote of bitter air find its way into her bloodstream. Her hand moved absently in the lines of a *magia* sigil. Warmth glowed deep inside, where the shudders of sleeplessness and revulsion moved.

A sudden spurt of voices broke her concentration.

Cold rushed in, tingling at her fingers' ends, and she raised her head, looking away from Pollexfen Calmady.

"Mistress Guillaime!" Abjectly enthusiastic, Bevil Calmady, bright in azure satin against the trodden mud and snow, offered his hand to assist the young woman back up the steps of the coach.

The White Crow abruptly stepped away, putting yards between herself and the boy's father. She pulled her cloak over her doublet. Her knuckles tightened: white. Apology, appeal: all of this on her face before she could control her expression.

All gone unnoticed.

Clutching her oversize black coat about her thin body, laughing, Desire-of-the-Lord Guillaime tottered across the snow on borrowed, two-inch-heeled shoes a size too large. Cold reddened her cheeks and lips, made her dark eyes sparkle. She called something up to Abiathar, visible now at the coach-window, and put one bruised hand up to her sleek and curly black hair. Caught up on the crown of her narrow head, hairpins falling out, hair unravelled down; and she pushed at it and lost her grip on her coat, that swung wide. Layers of skirts flew.

A rough voice swore in a whisper. The White Crow recognised it minutes later as Pollexfen Calmady's. Bevil Calmady froze. The young woman's head whipped around.

Hollow-eyed, bruised, pinched with fear: she for one second faced him, long lashes soot against suddenly sallow-green skin. She stumbled clumsily up the steps and into the coach. The slamming door cut off a querulous, waking mutter from Baltazar Causaubon.

The White Crow walked on, past the horses. She stood staring into distance across the white moorland until the cold mottled her bare hands purple and blue, and her empty stomach growled.

A dry-mouthed thirst drove her back to the gentlemen-mercenaries around the fire.

Ten miles north of London the column shouldered a massive hill and the view of the London basin opened up: a thick green tide of forest washing up to the edges of the hills.

"There!" Bevil Calmady stabbed a pointing finger.

Riders plunged away towards woodland cover. The sun glinted from burgonet helms, breastplates, and the barrels of pistols. Maybe a dozen men. One rider lagging at the rear spurred viciously and uselessly at his straining horse.

"Oh, lord." Gadsbury leaned and spat over his horse's shoulder. He chuckled. "There's always one lackwit. Look at him—*Bevil!*"

"They're Protectorate men!"

Bevil spurred his horse raw. The downhill grassland jolted past him, cold wind whipping his eyes; and he struggled to ease the hilt of the sword in his hand, the guards bruising his knuckles as the blade slipped.

The other mount and rider spurred on.

Bevil swung the sword up, coming within bare distance; skidded his horse around in a turn that all but foundered it; cut a backstroke slash that hit nothing at all; and was away before the enemy rider could turn.

A sudden rush of sound. Bess and Gadsbury rode past him, pounding across the frost-slippery grass, yelling as high as baying hounds. He spun his horse back to follow them.

"Stand, you whoreson, *stand!*" A deep voice belled desperation. *"Hold the line!"*

Enough sense penetrated his wind-blasted brain to know that there was no line, no battle, nothing but a skirmish; himself way out in front, the riders near the woods about to turn, one lifting his arm . . .

The flat *crack!* of a pistol echoed across the morning.

Bess and Gadsbury reined in, deliberately and visibly
leaving the pursuit. Across the hillside, the enemy force
vanished.

"I—"

He turned in the saddle and the sky blackened.

The smell of pain dizzied him, a smell like cracked glass.
He took his hands away from his face, unaware that he had
covered it. Dark red blood ran across his skin. Cold stung
his mashed lips and nose. He snuffled blood, staring.

"*That*," Pollexfen Calmady shouted, "is the wound you
should have got to teach you skirmishing is no game. Never
go in without support, *never* go in without orders: what do
I have to *do*, boy?"

Bevil removed a patched handkerchief from his pocket
and cupped it over his nose. Cold dried the blood on his
gloves and bare wrists.

Muffled, he said, "I'm sorry . . . Gadsbury, I'm sorry."

"No harm done. Spirits," the small man said gruffly, riding up; and Bess, Lady Winslow, added, "High spirits, he'll
lose that soon enough. Or at any rate, as soon as we do."

"Then let him learn some devil-damned responsibility!
Boy, you do the business attendant on this, and I'll check
on your handling of it later."

"Yes, Fa—yes, Captain."

Back in column, Bevil Calmady in turn rode beside each
of the company's two sergeants, listing point-duty and necessary extra guard duties for the night.

In mid-speech he looked up to see the White Crow's eyes
on him, the woman obviously listening; and no distaste in
her expression, only memory and a kind of self-mocking
hunger.

IV

The spiked heads on poles on Southwark bridge muttered their rote litanies of confession into the winter air.

White Crow glanced up at snow-crusted scalps and moving, blackened lips.

"The old place hasn't changed, I see."

Snow clung to stanchions. Below, Thamys froze, cracking barges in the slow grip of ice. Iron-rimmed coach-wheels rumbled on the bridge, sudden sparks striking in the cold afternoon.

"It won't change. Not until we rid ourselves of the cause."

Mud crusted the hems of the young woman's skirts. Desire walked with her hands tucked up into her sleeves, grey coat billowing. The cold air reddened her cheeks, the marks on her face, at least, beginning to fade after three days. A sepia bruise darkened the lower lid of one eye.

Straight-backed, the White Crow leaned the reins against the dapple grey's neck, avoiding a sedan chair carried against the flow of traffic. The lead carrier muttered thanks, red-faced and sweating. The wigged Lady Justice in the chair made no acknowledgement.

"By cause, you mean the Qu—"

"I mean to speak nothing that would lead to my speaking in public." A sharp jerk of her head, black hair flying, in the direction of the spiked poles.

"Still a danger?"

"Oh, yes."

Saddle motion rocked her hips. The White Crow sat erect; momentarily touching the rein to the dapple-grey's neck and riding closer to the coach. Jared solemnly waved. She waved back. Cold froze her temples, but she did not pull her hood further down.

"You have a town-house," Desire-of-the-Lord Guillaime said.

"My grandfather built a house in Roseveare Court, near the convent gardens. Twenty years' neglect is long enough to turn it to a slum, I don't doubt."

"The General knew you'd come. She will have had it set in order."

"Will she now. What does she *want* with him? Why don't you ride, for God's sake?" Exasperation rasped in the White Crow's voice; vanished. "Unless you'd rather walk? It's as you will."

Gentlemen-mercenaries rode by twos and threes, red-and-blue silk velvets stark against the snow and traffic. Lord Gadsbury and Sir John Hay shared a mount; Arbella Lacey rode Bevil Calmady's gelding—the boy riding in the second coach—and Captain Pollexfen Calmady reached across from the saddle to the first coach's window, taking the Lord-Architect's flask and drinking deep, and passing it to Arbella. Curses and laughter from the rest of the troop floated back down the bridge.

Bells rang out from the far bank's clustered streets.

"What did I tell you?" The White Crow shifted in the saddle, eyeing the horizon behind them. White cloud scarfed the hills. "Safe until today. We shall have blizzards tonight."

"That's not well. You may need to travel. For *Regina* Carola. And you must come to court—the Protector-General's court."

"I haven't agreed to anything yet!"

"Tomorrow. And him, too: the renegade architect."

The White Crow snuffled a small laugh. "Casaubon, a renegade?"

"Madam, if he helps us build the eye of the sun, every royalist will call him renegade. I think with good reason."

"You're an odd one, you."

The young woman shrugged, moving shoulders and elbows in a gesture that managed to indicate crowded southern streets, ice-locked quays, solemn Tower, mineshafts, temples, and all.

"I know the town," she said. "It's a grave and gallant city."

Tiny bells jingled on a white mule's harness. One of the child-priests of the Sun rode down the centre of the bridge. The White Crow drew her mount aside, in the coach's wake, waiting until he passed.

The black-haired young woman rested a hand on the mount's stirrup. Ungloved, her flesh marbled blue and purple with cold. The White Crow watched her receive pain.

"Desire—"

"It is my discipline. Suffering mitigates."

"I don't *believe*—!"

Dark eyes flicked up, the contact of gazes like a punch in the stomach. "Sin is the flesh. Sin is the failure to defend. The failure to achieve."

The White Crow glanced ahead at the lead coach. Casaubon's voice boomed, the higher registers of Arbella and Bess replying. She frowned. Between the ranks of poles lining the bridge, fragments of confessions drift down from dead withered lips:

"*—treason against her most Catholic Majesty Carola. Second of that name—*"

"*—the rack, and then drawn on a hurdle to this place—*"

"—*against the Protector, Olivia, this sin*—"

"—*pain*—"

"—*for crows to peck at, as a warning*—"

She snorted in black amusement.

"I'll do what you want."

"Yes." Desire-of-the-Lord Guillaime tucked her bare hand back into her armpit. "I thought you would."

"Tell me, is it me, or are you enjoying this?"

The young woman limped, heeled boots skidding on the bridge's trodden snow. The White Crow looked down at her unprotected bare head, tangled matt-black hair; reached down with one hand that she drew back with the movement hardly begun.

Desire lifted her face to the low afternoon sunlight. Cheeks red, eyes brilliant with cold. A transparent drop of moisture hung delicate at her nostril. For the first time that the White Crow could remember, her lips moved in a smile.

"Oh, yes."

The White Crow rode silent all the way to Roseveare House.

"There's our old inn, *The Greene Lyon*," Bess Winslow suggested, as cautiously as if she handled wild gorse. "It's that or take Protectorate quarters."

"You're quartermaster, do as you will."

Pollexfen Calmady's voice rumbled, half-inaudible, his chin down in the lace at his throat.

Night blurred the fine edges of the winter afternoon. Roofs, weathercocks, towers, and gables all faded into sepia. Her horse's hooves crunched through the snow's ice-rime, grimy with coal dust. She glanced behind her at the company riding; bright plumes dimmed in a Protectorate street. They kept no perceptible distance between themselves and the older Calmady.

She said, "You know I follow you."

His head lifted. The creases of his face deepened as he

smiled. He made a small sound in the back of his throat: amusement or cynicism or merely acknowledgement. "*The Greene Lyon*, then. And devil take the hindmost for a night's work—drinking!"

She looked at Gadsbury, close behind Calmady, and the other mercenaries. "Count me in with you!"

Rising in the east, a piss-yellow moon stained the sky.

Sweat slicked her cheek.

Half asleep, she fumbled a fold of the sheet under her face and let it mop up the film of heat. Casaubon's flesh shifted under her, solidly warm.

She lay belly-down across the vast expanse of the Lord-Architect's hips, back, and shoulders; pillowed against the fat of his bolster-arms, her nose buried in the curly, short hair at the nape of his neck. Slightly rank flesh smelled warm in her nostrils. Rhythmic, untroubled breathing lifted her.

". . . Mmrhhnn?"

Belly on back, sweat-glued to every contour of muscle under pillows of fat, she shifted one leg; her pubis resting on the cool flesh of his buttock, a foot trailing down to the bed. Heat and slick sweat woke her, and the frost-cold air that touched her unprotected ear outside the blanket.

Awkwardly, peeling skin from skin, she slid down into the folds of blankets tenting his body, and yelped at the touch of cold cloth.

". . . *time* is 't?'"

The White Crow hitched herself up against sloping pillows, grabbing at sheets to bundle round her bare shoulders. Brilliant, the morning light of heavy snowfall gleamed on every polished wood panel and candlestick of the room. Her breath huffed silver-grey. "Wake up, rot you! It's late. General Olivia."

"She can *wait*. So can t'other."

The bedframe creaked loudly. The fat man, nose still bur-

ied in linen, reached one ham-hand up to grab blankets and
rolled massively over onto his side; hunched down so that
only a tuft of copper-red hair showed.

"Ei!" The White Crow hugged her bare breasts, left on
the naked and blanket-denuded side of the bed.

"You should be *up!*" She hit the cloth-covered bulk, fist
bouncing back from solidity. The Lord-Architect Casaubon
rolled over onto his other side, in the bed that shifted on
the floorboards and squeaked in protest, and rested his chins
on his hand. Dark red lashes lifted. He beamed sleepily at
her.

"I am," he said, "I am . . ."

Momentarily taken aback, she blinked and then grinned.
"Good."

She ran her finger over the fullness of his lower lip, down
his underlip to the deep swell of his chin. Soft against the
pad of her finger: delicate flesh and moist breath.

Humour retreated, burned up by something more urgent
in his eyes. His free hand slid across under the blankets and
pulled her sprawling against his body. She dug fingers deep
into his capacious flesh, wrestling, blind in the sweat and
odour of desire; too urgent now to do anything but take.

The Lord-Architect Casaubon flicked open his court fan with
a practised twist of the wrist. He eyed himself in his mirror
over the black-painted, sequin-decorated sealskin, flirted an
eyebrow, and gave a beam that the fan concealed.

"Perfect!" he announced. "Ah. Little one . . ."

"Mmm?"

He turned from the full-length mirror. Outside the window, in Roseveare Court, a yellowing sky bled snow. Against
this light, the Master-Physician White Crow bent to buckle
the fifth chain-and-buckle on her left boot.

"Is that entirely wise?"

The woman straightened. She hooked a pair of thin iron
chains from her belt, over her narrow black leather trousers,
looping through the crotch and twisting to fasten them at

her hip. Other chains tautened: at hip, knee, calf, and ankle. She put one hand to her cinnamon-coloured hair, braids fastened up with black-iron clips.

"Formal plain black. That's what you wear at the Protectorate court. Puritan black. I know these things, remember? I was born here."

She laced the black leather bodice more tightly over her breasts, and tucked a black rose into their visible division. The bodice's straps cut into her bare arms. A studded collar circled her throat. A black-hilted dagger clinked, dangling from one thigh.

"And if the General should happen to *suspect* that I don't much like the puritan Protectorate—or being hauled out of Roseveare on business that isn't mine—or being emotionally blackmailed by her messenger Desire Guillaime—well, then: good!"

The Lord-Architect drew himself up to his full six-foot-five, weight back on one heeled shoe, black brocade coat swirling. He flicked the sealskin fan closed and secreted it away in an inside pocket. The immense turned-back cuffs of the coat snagged on the black-silk embroidery of his waistcoat and breeches.

"Sometimes, Master-Physician, you're just plain embarrassing company."

"Ha!"

The White Crow slung a glove-soft leather cloak around her shoulders and pulled on black leather gauntlets. Her turn arrested partway: she stared herself up and down in Casaubon's mirror. "I'm really going to go out on the streets like this, just to make a point about Olivia's self-styled puritans? No! Yes. I suppose I am. Let's go, before I lose whatever nerve I have left."

Window-glass vibrated. A lump of decaying snow slid down. The Lord-Architect paced across creaking bare boards, opened the window, and gazed down into the snow-choked narrow street. Lamps burned in the row of booksellers' shop-windows along Roseveare Court. "It's Guillaime."

Her hand pushed his arm. He moved back. She leaned over the casement, looking down at the girl in her layers of skirts and coats. Snow settled and melted in black hair.

"I've called your carriage." Snow distanced Desire-of-the-Lord's voice.

The Lord-Architect nodded ponderously. Beside him, White Crow lifted a hand in acknowledgement and pulled the window quickly closed.

"I'll have to find time to examine her today. She's healing well. Bodily. What's in her mind . . . *I don't know!* I suppose I can at least tell her if she has pox or a bastard."

"Little one, don't be so bitter."

"Oh, that's the strange thing. I'm not."

The White Crow walked to the bassinet, lifting out the baby with automatic care. She nuzzled her face against it.

"Are you coming with us, then? Little Jadis? Coming to see what lunacy we're about to be roped into?"

"Yawp!"

The Lord-Architect Casaubon thoughtfully picked up two spare feeding bottles of milk, tucking them into one outside pocket, and slid a handful of rusks into the other. He licked crumbs from his gloved fingers. Milk oozed into the black cloth.

"Father!"

The Lord-Architect gazed around the small, panelled chamber. His gaze abruptly lowered. A beam spread over his face. Jared, in the doorway, and spruce in brown frock-coat and breeches, eyed his father with long-suffering patience.

"Father, why don't you let Abiathar carry those?"

Casaubon slowly squatted down on his haunches. Level with Jared's face, he met puzzled blue eyes.

"Abiathar is taking *you* to see the sights of the town. Won't that be nice?"

The eight-year-old clasped hands behind his back and frowned disapprovingly. "I *would* like to go to the Stock Market, Father. And the 'Change, if I may."

The Lord-Architect Casaubon raised his eyes. The woman

shook her head, mouthing a sentence which he deciphered as *Nothing on* my *side of the family.* With some effort, he rose to his feet.

"Of course you may. Tell Abiathar that I said so."

The door shut soundlessly behind Jared.

"No," Casaubon said, "*I* don't know where he gets it from, either."

"It's safer than taking him to court."

The redhaired woman rested Jadis in the crook of her arm, swaddled in a woollen coat and her own cloak; walking towards the door. Chains jingled. She shot the Lord-Architect a speaking look. Casaubon shut his mouth. He followed her down narrow, winding flights of stairs. Snow-light shone yellow at casements and high clerestory windows. A tiny bell chimed, another, and two more: the clocks of Roseveare House striking ten in the morning, in anything but unison.

"At least one of those struck seventeen." He reached past her in the narrow hall to open the door.

"I'm worried."

"We can call in a clock-mender. In fact, I myself have some degree of talent in that respect—"

"*Not* about the clocks!"

"I know. I have also some degree of talent as regards the noble craft of architecture. Count on me to content this Protector-General."

The door swung half-open and lodged. A wall of cold air hit him in the face. The Lord-Architect drew his foot back and kicked the door. The door banged open and back against the house wall. Congealed snow and ice spanged off the shopfronts across the street. A patch of snow slid off the opposite roof and fell six floors to pock the street beneath. The Lord-Architect blinked.

"*Ca*saubon . . ."

He slid gilt-and-sequined buttons into three-inch button-holes, fastening the black brocade frock-coat up to his chins. White flakes blew in and settled on his sleeves. He turned the coat-collar up.

"You'd better take this." From the tail-pocket of the coat, he retrieved a metal flask and handed it to the cloaked woman, beaming hopefully. "Pure alcohol. No smell on your breath! Keep you warm, though."

He leaned out, looking towards the end of the street. Wrapped in coats, in snow deep enough to hide her heeled boots, Desire-of-the-Lord Guillaime stood by a closed carriage. Percherons in black drapes breathed plumes of steam into the cold air.

The Lord-Architect Casaubon, moving a step lower down, clumsily wrapped his arms around White Crow and baby both. He kissed her.

"We shall be received separately at court, I take it. The Guillaime woman your sponsor. And Polly Calmady, mine."

Towards mid-morning the falling snow obscured the upper storeys of the White Tower and the spire of St. Peotyr's Chapel. Yellow cloud pressed low. Smoke whipped up and down from chimneys, fraying into the wind.

Shuddering against cold, Pollexfen Calmady stared through the whirling particles. Arbella Lacey and Calmady's son escorted the White Crow rapidly into the White Tower, towards warmth; the redhaired woman huddled about her baby.

The Lord-Architect stepped away from the carriage, heels crunching down the snow and ice. In his gloved hands he held the handle of an immense black umbrella. A few specks of snow blasted under the gabardine to cling to his unprotected hair and the shoulders of the black brocade frock-coat.

"She won't interview me out here, I trust?"

"Here comes the bitch-General now."

Men and women, heads down, plunged from the shelter of the chapel. Snow crunched under heavy boots. Black cassocks and robes, torn at by the wind, flared open; black dresses scuffed up clinging wet sleet. A heavy figure stomped in the lead, the obscure morning light glinting from black steel breastplate and gauntlets; striding without pause across the grassy patch—hidden under a foot of virgin snow—of Tower Green.

Pollexfen Calmady called, "Madam!"

The armoured woman lifted a hand in acknowledgement. She raised her head, looking up into the bite of the wind, eyes narrowed. "The White Tower, if you please, Captain."

He nodded, striding after the Protector-General, among the black-clad and silent men and women, clattering up the steps to the tower's entrance. The Lord-Architect walked unsteadily across the treacherous stones of the yard after him, at the arched doorway, folding his umbrella, shaking it vigorously over assembled Protectorate soldiers, and entering with a film of snow melting on his coat and head.

Pollexfen Calmady removed his plumed hat and shook out the curls of his periwig.

"Madam General—"

The Protector-General Olivia halted, a short distance into the crowded hall.

He glanced ahead, following her gaze. The Lord-Architect's wife stood, cloak now thrown back, holding the baby up under its arms, rubbing her cheek to the child's.

She carried her weight on the balls of her feet. Chains and belts jingled, slung on diagonals across her taut hips, encased in sober black leather. Her skin gleamed in the dark room: black rose wound into the fastenings of her tight bodice. Black-iron studs ringed her wrists; clipped up her spice-red hair.

Pollexfen Calmady surprised himself with laughter. "A scandal to the view, and without infringing even *one* of the sumptuary laws—Madam White Crow, my congratulations."

She raised innocent brows.

Olivia's weather-hardened voice cut across low gossip. "You would be more comfortable in another room, madam; there are fires, and I would not have your child take cold. Captain Calmady, escort her."

Pollexfen Calmady bowed, a movement calculatedly just too precise for the Protectorate court. "Certainly, madam."

His gaze followed the General for a moment: a small woman, brushing snow from her wool cloak, followed towards the guardroom-office by the Lord-Architect. The black-clothed court shifted out of the way of the fat man's oblivious progress.

"This way," he said to the man's wife.

As he turned, he saw in snow-yellow light a young woman, black-haired and swathed in layers of skirts, who followed the Protector-General as far as the guardroom door.

The Protector unbuckled her gauntlets and held her hands out to the fire. She looked over her shoulder. Morning's subdued illumination touched her wispy hair, bulbous features, and eyes the colour of light. Her weathered complexion put her anywhere between forty and fifty: a woman not plain, but ugly.

"Master architect."

He hooked his furled umbrella over one immense arm, and made a flourishing bow. "Baltazar Casaubon."

"And the woman with the child—your wife?" Without waiting for acknowledgement, the small woman went on: "I cannot like her dress. And yet I like the humour of it."

The fat man beamed. "My thought exactly!"

"As to your task—"

She stepped to the scrubbed guardroom table and unrolled the first of a set of blueprints.

Spidered in thin lines, the skeleton of a temple rose over the city. A great columned temple from which a white dome would rise, its topmost span open to the noon sun. The Lord-Architect reached down one fat finger and turned the paper slightly, aligning it to compass-points.

"The site was chosen for you, by necessity . . ." He squinted. The rolls of fat on his cheeks almost hid his china-blue eyes. "And the time of construction, also?"

"I am given to understand dire portents if the building is not completed this summer two years on."

"And you have what?"

"The foundations and some lower walls."

"Nothing of the dome?"

"Nothing. What is built, collapses."

He fumbled in an inside pocket and extracted a small steel rule. While bending over the plan and measuring scale, he murmured, "How many other master-masons have you called in on this?"

"Two. One's dead, one is not dead yet—she being confined to Bedlam, and so like to die eventually. Does that dishearten you, master architect?"

Copper-gold eyebrows flicked up: he glanced at her and returned to the plans.

"Then I shall add dead workmen, to the number of five, all expert in their craft; more accidents than can be criminally accounted for; a site no man will approach after dusk; and there you have the truth of it."

The Lord-Architect snapped the steel rule shut and tucked it back into his pocket. He straightened his back cautiously. "And the eye of the sun has been building, what, three years?"

"All of that during period of the truce."

"Under the Protectorate."

"The worse for us if we confess a failure now. The godless monarch Carola will make much capital from it." Olivia reached across, rolled up the plans, and presented them to him across her buff-coated arm, as one presents a sword. "Suitable rewards, for success. Upon failure, follows—nothing but that I try again with another architect. Doubting, sir, that you will have survived, more than the first two, if you fail in this."

"So *let* the Guillaime bitch complain."

Arbella Lacey leaned back across the Florentine cannon in the Ordnance, one knee up, boot supported against its iron wheel. She picked under her black nails with a dagger.

"There's fourteen of us to swear an oath you never touched her, Captain. No, nor never even thought on it."

"And the fifteenth?"

The big woman shrugged, her gaze dropping from his. Pollexfen Calmady smiled.

Down the ranked cannon, that stood displayed now in the vaulted halls, the gentlemen-mercenaries stood in groups: bright as oriels among the black dress of the Protectorate. Calmady looked for his son. A boy with curling fair hair to his shoulders, in silver lace and blue satin; the worst excesses of his dress curbed.

"Gadsbury has been tasking him over fashion, I perceive." Pollexfen Calmady tugged his long scarlet coat straight. "Well, will you wager with me on how large a bonus the bitch-General *won't* give us, for swift completion of her request?"

Muted sun shone in on the scrubbed floorboards, and on the whitewashed vaults of the ceiling. Outside the arrow-slit windows, he glimpsed the snow-shrouded Bloody Tower, and flakes swirling to hide the heads above Traitors Gate. Loud footsteps broke his concentration.

"Master Calmady."

"That is Captain Calmady, Master Humility, as I hope to give you cause to remember."

"Sir." Humility Talbot bowed a frozen inch. Black coat, hose, and stockings; not a silver buckle to his shoes, or a silver top to his cane. He sniffed, as if at some odour. "He has accepted her commission—you may escort the Protector-General's architect home."

Pollexfen Calmady whistled sharply, once, through his teeth. Arbella Lacey slid to the floor, lithely dangerous; Gadsbury and Lord Rule appeared out of the crowd. Heads turned.

Calmady let one hand fall to his sword-hanger, the weight of metal at his hip a reassurance and an enjoyment. Seeing the scandal in Humility Talbot's expression, he smiled the wider; swept his plumed hat off and made a low leg. Something in the cold air, the unornamented walls, or the isolation of the mercenary troop at this court of black daws, made a shiver walk the bones of his back.

"Talbot, my orders are given by the General herself. I

would be obliged, sir, if you would take your rotten carcass out of the way while I receive them."

The crop-haired man snorted, turned his back, and stalked off.

General Olivia closed the small room's door behind her as she entered. The redhaired woman looked up from the hearth-seat, where she sat by the fire, baby cradled in her lap. Olivia gazed for a moment.

"I see you don't carry a sword. I understood you to be a Scholar-Soldier."

The woman put one foot up on the seat. Thin black-iron chains jingled; leather creaked. She grinned. Infectious: the skin around her eyes creased with warmth.

"Promoted Master-Physician, madam Protector. Does that make me useless for what you have in mind?"

"Not, I think you may regret to hear, necessarily."

Olivia brushed wispy yellow-grey hair out of her eyes. She dropped her unbuckled back- and breastplate behind the door with a hefty clash of metal, crossed to the writing-desk, and slumped into the chair. Ignoring piled-up parchments requiring signature, she steepled her gnarled fingers and rested her chin on them. She studied the magus.

"You have a child."

"I have two."

"Nor that, neither, would not have prevented me calling on your assistance. You're Roseveare—how is it you like to be called now? Valentine? Or Crow, is it?"

"White Crow."

"Mmm."

Olivia laughed: a gruff, flat sound that surprised her in the snow-muffled air. A cold draught blew across her shins.

"Unsurprisingly, then, I would use the crow as my messenger bird. You know Carola."

"I haven't seen the woman since—"

"Since your twelfth birthday. In the Banqueting Hall, the night of *The Masque of Death and Diamonds*."

"Now how the hell did you know that?"

The woman reached down, picking the black rose out of her bodice and placing it on the bench beside her. Fire heated her skin to rose. Fingers unlacing the leather, she lifted the half-sleeping baby to her nipple. It sucked.

"Not that I suppose it matters. Your little girl—your messenger, Guillaime—told me, General. You want Carola in exile. Now, for one thing, the Invisible College doesn't get involved in civil revolt. For another, I hold no brief for the Queen *or* the Protectorate. And for a third . . ."

"Enough."

Olivia slid down in the carved chair. Black hessian cloth galled her shoulders. She scratched at her nose, and then snapped her fingers. A servant entered silently with a tray of tea and sweatmeats.

"The Invisible College frequently interferes." She waved the man away, and poured tea. The golden liquid steamed. "I don't care about your loyalties, either. I have all the loyal people I can well cope with, mistress magus. For once, I would deal with someone who understands plain dealing and advantage."

She paused, testing the liquid's temperature with her finger against the side of the cup. The fire crackled. From outside, flat in the snow-filled air, came the clash of troops drilling in the bailey.

"I would be perfectly happy to go on fighting this civil revolt with mercenary troops. Why bleed my commonwealth to death? The false ruler Carola thinks differently. She'd rouse us all to fight. Well, we have this amnesty now, and the royalists know how badly they're placed: it's no secret. So, if funded, the Queen might flee into exile."

"Funded?"

"Afer civil revolt, all of us are poor; but I have control of the town's funds, while I hold the town."

Olivia sipped at the cup. Still too hot, the tea scalded her lips. She snorted, put it aside, and sat up. A rummage among the papers excavated a previously drawn-up commission. She tossed it to the redhaired woman.

"Roseveare doesn't have any money."

"*Carola* doesn't know that. I'm a plain woman. I won't use subterfuge with you. Here is a draft for six thousand guineas. Take it to the Mint: the Master of the Mint will let you have coin. Take the coin to Carola, persuade her to take it on what pretext you will. Then go home to your estate. And stay untouched by the commonwealth's troubles."

She watched the woman. A vagueness in the tawny eyes she put down to the nursing child; not deceived by it.

"Or else not?"

"Or else not," Olivia confirmed. "No penalties."

"Anybody could do this. Why me?"

" 'Anybody' did not meet the godless Queen Carola at *The Masque of Death and Diamonds*. Nor 'anybody' has not been out of the commonwealth these twenty years, close on, and so is part of no faction."

She swept the cup up and drained it at a gulp. Standing, she moved to the window. Specks of snow whirled black against the clouds. Faces, shapes, trees, demons, battles: all visible in that mutable white. From behind her, the husky voice said:

"I take it the Protectorate's grip on the capital isn't secure, but it's secure enough to lay hands on anyone *other* than Carola absconding with six thousand guineas?"

"I assure you."

Warmth and movement at her buff-coated elbow: Olivia glanced sideways to find the woman beside her at the window. The baby, swaddled and up against a black-leather shoulder, burped. The Master-Physician Valentine Roseveare stared out through the leaded glass.

"If I can't persuade her?"

"No harm to you or yours. I'm not vindictive. If truth were told, I hold this as having one chance in five of success;

enough to make it a worthy attempt. I would save future
bloodshed, if I could."

Creases crinkled around the woman's eyes. The faintest
rose-pale illumination clung to her skin: a reflection from
the child's red-orange hair. Olivia reached out and rubbed
at the frost-patterns on the glass.

"Then you understand—"

Sudden laughter sounded by the hearth. She looked over
her shoulder. An unsubstantial boy of perhaps ten, in an
antique velvet suit, played with a rough-coated dog beside
the fire. His ghostly elder, a brother some twelve or fourteen years old, looked down and laughed. The White-rose
badges of Princes hung on chains around their spectral
necks. The elder boy wore a circlet of gold around his brow.

"General—!"

"Holding court in the Tower has notable disadvantages.
Take no notice. It's a common occurrence. Tell me if I have
your agreement to this enterprise?"

Olivia took the woman's arm and turned her back to the
window. Behind her, the laughter faded. Before it quite
crossed the verge of hearing it became smothered: screaming began.

"I've seen women—*and* men—raped with knives. With broken bottles! Cut, butchered. Women raped by half a company, and then murdered. Male soldiers sodomised. The
blood's hot after battles, so . . . *that's* rape."

Pollexfen Calmady put his fists on his hips. Turned-back
satin cuffs shone scarlet. He glared across the crowded audience hall, following the Lord-Architect Casaubon's gaze.

Bevil Calmady, with Gadsbury and the White Crow, stood
waiting by the main door for the carriage.

"How can I ever be a boy again?" His breath clouded the
air with a scent of alcohol. One puritan courtier drew back;
he sneered.

"Too much happens to us, Baltazar. And we do too much,
ourselves. Men have their peccadillos; if he's weak-

stomached—man, what am I going to do! For a piece of woman-flesh to come between me and my son . . ."

He shook his head. The periwig's loose ringlets flew.

"If I were you," Baltazar Casaubon said, "I'd discover what he says now to your lieutenant Gadsbury."

Pollexfen Calmady nodded. The icy air coming in with the continual opening and shutting of the doors breathed across his face, the skin fever-hot. The Tower's stone smelled dank. Hushed voices echoed between the white-washed walls.

He stared wistfully up at the nearest arrow-slit window and the falling flakes.

"I was born on an estate of three hundred and sixty-five fountains dedicated to the moon . . . A place in the mountains. Bevil, also. He left too young to recall it. Gambled away. Some city bitch has it now."

"Polly—"

The creases in his lined face deepened. His voice sounded harsh. "I got myself into this one. No one had to do it for me. But, *fortuna imperatrix mundi*. I gambled away estate and wealth, tell me I'm not about to gamble away my boy."

Two strides away he checked, turned, and added, "Not a word to him. I tried to weep for it. My eyes are dry."

He jostled a cassock-clad man aside and pushed between two crop-haired women, ignoring their pious curses. A neigh echoed from the yard beyond the White Tower's doors. Blue-grey light flooded in with a snarl of fine snow as the doors opened.

"Gadsbury, is he telling you what I conceive he is?" He caught the boy's blue-satin sleeve. "Don't be a fool."

"I'm leaving the company, Father."

Air rushed into his lungs, only the bitter hurt of that to tell him that his breathing faltered. Pollexfen Calmady coughed. He looked down at the flagstones, seeing fine snow whisk about his boots. And raised his eyes to stare at the young man's pale, determined face.

"In Christ's name, why!"

A stir in the crowd made him step aside automatically; not until then registering that the Protector and her entourage were coming through.

"Why? All I've heard from you—" he dropped his voice to a rough whisper— "since I took you from your mother's pap, all I've heard from you is *gentleman-mercenary*. Why alter your course now?"

The self-possessed young man met his eyes. In blue satin and ice-lace, as incongruous among these black courtiers as a jay; straight-backed and slender, one hand on the hilt of his sword.

"I'll join another company. Any other company."

"Boy." His face twisted.

The Lord-Architect's voice boomed as he passed through the door with White Crow; something about the carriage; and Pollexfen Calmady glanced up automatically.

Silhouetted against the blue outdoor light, a young woman stood with her bare hands tucked up into her armpits. Head bowed, boots neatly together; the topmost of her skirts a ragged black, and her topcoat grey. Without raising her head, she turned it; glittering eyes meeting his.

Pollexfen Calmady rested his hand on Bevil's shoulder. "Madam Protector!"

The plain-faced woman slowed, fingers of her left hand busy buckling a gauntlet, her head cocked to hear another man read her a report as she walked. "Captain Calmady? There is something more?"

Light from the slit-windows reflected from his eyes: a gaze with some manic glint of humour or despair, impossible to detect which.

"There is one more thing," he said. "There has, or there will be, a complaint of a rape laid against my name. Will you allow me to be tried and cleared of it?"

Bevil Calmady opened his mouth, shut it again.

The Protector squinted against the subdued lamps and snow-bright morning. "Who lays the complaint?"

"Desire-of-the-Lord Guillaime is her name."

Feet shuffled. He looked over his shoulder. Without a word, and as one, the men and women of the Protectorate court drew back, until a clear space of flagstones surrounded the black-haired young woman. She lifted her head. The light brought out the faded bruise under her eye.

Humility Talbot whispered, "A soiled woman is the abomination of desolation spoken of by the prophet . . ."

"Desire-of-the-Lord, is it so?"

"Yes."

Sullen, her low voice sounded clearly in the quiet.

"Then you're arrested, Captain Calmady, and your trial will follow." The Protector briefly signalled, and did not wait to watch the helmeted guards move in to surround Calmady. Desire-of-the-Lord Guillaime hugged her arms more tightly about her body, standing alone.

"Father."

Guards grabbed his shoulders. Pollexfen Calmady shrugged loose, nodded to Bevil, and walked with a jaunty step between the armed men, halting as he passed Arbella Lacey.

"Trooper."

He dug in his pocket, slid a rattle of silver coin from his hand into hers.

"Take that down to Bankside. Get the best odds you can. I want to lay the heaviest wager possible that I'll be acquitted."

V

The White Crow straightened up from tucking a torn rag into the crack between wall and floorboard. She held her hand out for a moment, testing for cold draughts.

"That's one dangerous woman: Olivia. She looks like a farmer on her way to plough a field . . . and you agree to what she proposes without even *thinking* about it. Not that I'm well-placed against threats, with children."

The Lord-Architect cocked an eyebrow.

"Oh, well enough, then; *we* aren't well-placed!" She pulled the nearest rug up to the clothes-chest, overlapping it, and sat back on her heels as Jared entered.

"Mama, Abiathar said it was too *time-consuming* to travel around town and see things. She let me visit the shops in the court, to buy whatever I wanted." Jared, in stocking-feet and without his coat, maneuvered armsful of papers carefully in and shut the door. "I have *all* today's newspapers."

"Ah." The White Crow watched him trot across and settle in a deep armchair. "Ah. Good. I suppose. Casaubon, they won't be building in this weather, will they?"

"Hardly." The Lord-Architect inclined his head with ponderous grace.

She kicked the rug across to the hearth, and spread the bed-quilt over it. A last check between door and hearth, window and hearth; and she knelt down to take the baby from the bassinet.

"So you can look after these two while I go out."

The orange-haired baby, unwound from swaddling wool clothes, stretched her limbs in crab-like movements, hitching herself facedown across the blanket in an approximation of a crawl.

The Lord-Architect Casaubon appeared miffed. "The Protector-General won't take kindly to my delaying."

"Nor me, either—"

"I must go to the site sometime today."

"*Mama!*"

The White Crow, standing up, grunted as she received Jared's full weight in her midriff. The boy clung, his arms tightly round her waist.

"You're going away again!"

She met Casaubon's gaze across the room. Obscurely warmed, she scruffled Jared's neat blond hair. "No I'm not, pudding. Promise."

"You *are.*"

The White Crow bent from the knee, closed her arm across the boy's thighs, and with a grunt of effort hoisted him into her arms. She looked at his red face, level now with hers, and kissed his cheek.

"All I'm doing, pudding, is going somewhere perfectly respectable for the afternoon, if I can get through the streets."

Her head cocked to one side, she suddenly grinned. The boy wriggled. As if recollecting his dignity, he slid to the floor and pulled his cut-down waistcoat straight. The White Crow squatted down on her haunches.

"Can we trust your papa to look after Jadis on his own, do you think?"

The small boy's gaze shifted to Casaubon. Before he could voice his obvious doubts, the White Crow concluded: "How would you like to come with me on a visit to the Mint?"

Jared frowned seriously.

"I would like that very much, mama." He hesitated. "If you take me, then *you* won't look sus . . . suspicious, will you?"

The White Crow whistled, and looked across at Casaubon. The Lord-Architect's chins creased in a vastly amused beam.

"An infant after my own heart!"

She held out her hand, waited until Jared took it, and pulled him into a hug. "But he's perfectly right."

Desire-of-the-Lord Guillaime sat waiting for him in one of *The New-Founde Land Arms*'s high-backed cubicles. Sir Denzil Waldegrave, seating himself opposite her with customary insouciance, noted first something brittle about her body language, and then the traces of bruises on her face.

He put his ale mug down with care. "One time, my little spy, you shall have to tell me why you do this."

The young woman looked at him with dark, dancing eyes. She hugged her greatcoat around herself. Snow melted in her hair. "Why? I suppose because it pleases me."

Denzil Waldegrave sprawled back, fingering ringlets. "No protestations of loyalties to myself, or to the Crown, or to the commonwealth? Merely, 'It pleases me'?"

Something shifted in her face. She looked down at her cold-mottled hands, shrouded in fingerless leather gloves.

"You've said often that you know 'my sort.' My lord."

Waldegrave shrugged. "You might say I have a sympathy with you. A Puritan girl for whom purity was too cold, and so she makes herself available to good Queen Carola's court, for sport or for advancement. Pardon my cynicism. I am a debatable case myself. No man—nor no woman neither—knows for sure who'll come out victor in this war."

"I care not, either way." Now her eyes did glow, but the humour had a new, bitter cast. "I amuse myself. My lord."

"Why, Desire, you're dangerous. Honest, and so therefore dangerous. A pretender, and so therefore dangerous. Joyful in a time of war, and so therefore dangerous."

THE ARCHITECTURE OF DESIRE

"Am I so?"

"You hide yourself from yourself, and are therefore dangerous—to yourself." Denzil Waldegrave drained his ale mug. "So: now. Without more delay. What word from that woman's court?"

"The sole news I have for my lord is this. She has her architect come to her from the provinces. He arrived yesterday. I'll tell you his name," the girl said, "and you can pay me your silver pennies later."

The bulk of the building cut off the rising wind. Snow crunched, giving underfoot. The White Crow stamped her boots down into the settled mass. Jared, brown coat neatly buttoned, trotted in her tracks.

"Mama, sometimes I think father isn't very responsible."

Her head went back. The White Crow gave a great bark of laughter. Jared stopped by the Royal Mint and Observatory's entrance and knocked the crushed snow off his boots. Cold flushed his cheeks red.

Snow covered the wide steps and the pillared portico. Squared Palladian roofs bore a weight of white. The glass of the observatory-dome glittered, each pane's snow thinning towards the centre, showing the light within.

"Mama?"

"I would say, don't underestimate your father, Jared—however, I suspect you're right. He *is* irresponsible. I've often said so myself."

"Oh, mama!"

The boy pushed his tricorne hat more squarely upon his head. He gazed up. The winged-dragon weathervane above the portico creaked around, bronze wings shrieking open, snow shaking down. It shrieked:

"Will you watch the skies?
Debase the coinage of lies?
New-mint a truth that we can know?
Will you enter? Will you forego?"

Jared lifted his hat politely. "Enter, if you please."

"Now." The White Crow knelt. Cold soaked the knee of her breeches. "Draw me the *magia*-sigil for finding your way back to Roseveare."

He raised stubby fingers and drew, stolidly, upon the air. A faint flare lightened the snow: the White Crow quenched it with a gesture of her own.

"And the sigil for people not to notice you're there? Good. And to call me or your father, if you should need us? Yes . . . more after this fashion. Thus. Yes. Good, Jarrie."

"I wish you wouldn't call me that, mama."

"You'll do."

Straightening, her hand fell to her hip. Her gloved hand brushed her studded doublet, under the thick frieze coat that hung open; no sword-belt and no blade.

One of the pair of vast wooden doors creaked open. Golden light slanted into the dim daylight. A blast of heat hit the White Crow's face, bringing awareness of how cold numbed her skin. She rested three fingers on Jared's shoulder, steering him towards the door: a mother and her child, visiting tourist sights. A smile crinkled the skin around her eyes, deepening delicate lines.

"Yes?" A stout man peered out, loose brown satin robe falling open to show a fine linen shirt. A long brown periwig fell halfway down his chest and back. "Madam?"

"White Crow, Master-Physician of the Invisible College. This is my son Jared. I'm told I can speak with the Master of the Mint, Master Isaac."

The man stared from under heavy eyebrows. A wide mouth and large nose made his oval face seem crowded of feature. He plucked absently at one of the periwig's trailing curls. His gaze fell on Jared.

"Ah, I see. An *educational* visit. I am Master Isaac, madam. Come in, come in. Be *quiet!*"

The dragon-weathervane cut off its chant in mid-shriek and pivoted north-north-east in a fit of pique. The White Crow grinned up at it. Boot-heels skidding in slush, she followed Jared through the entrance and into the warm corridors of the Royal Mint and Observatory. The door creaked shut behind them.

The boy stopped and stared around at the milling benches, the stone grinders, the cutters and clippers, and the baskets of coin that spilled across the floor. Workers glanced up at their entrance. Isaac signalled them to continue.

"Through this way, madam, if you please. We have a most interesting observation in progress."

The metallic din faded as they passed a further door. The White Crow automatically trod softly, staring up in dim light at the brass barrels and adjustment-cogs and wheels of a great telescope. Frost chilled the air, the glass observation-dome cranked open a yard or two.

"This most recent comet may now be viewed in daylight." Master Isaac bustled forward, a restraining hand on Jared's shoulder. "As you may see, madam. Young man, a comet is a collection of rocks and visible gases that circle the sun; not, as has been in error supposed, a celestial influence—"

Turning to the small lens-piece let her hide a smile. Behind her, the boy gave a forty-five-year-old man's dry cough.

She peered into the lens. Whiteness swung and focused in a bright blue sky. Magnified, the white dot swelled to a clear image.

A snarling lion's mask shone against the sky.

Dust-hazed, distinct, and of a marble whiteness: a hollow lion-head. Unbearable highlights shone on wrinkled lips, nostrils, on the great rigid swathes of mane; the light of the sun reflectant in purple-blue, oxygen-starved space. Intense indigo sky showed through the hollow eye-holes.

"That's Sekhmet's Comet."

Master Isaac's disembodied voice held surprise. "You're well-informed."

"After a fashion. It's not my specialist field."

Sunlight, unhindered by air and dust, blazed from the point of one white-marble canine tooth. Pitting and scoring marked the stone pelt: the abrasions of aeons. Corroded dust starred the great stone mane, trailing in the Lion-comet's wake with invisibly slow ripples.

She stood back, blinking, to let Jared at the lens. Through the edges of the observation dome, the comet reduced itself to a chalk-white smear across a patch of blue sky.

"Rocks and gases?"

"Any *apparent* shape is coincidental, madam, I assure you."

Her feet followed the man automatically, oblivious until she caught a door as it swung back and ushered Jared through in front of her into the milling room.

"I'll speak of the milling process itself in a moment, madam." The grey-wigged man gestured with restrained excitement, his eyes bright. "If I might prevail upon you for a moment, first, Master-Physician—this is something of my own. Young master Jared may find it intriguing."

"Yes," the woman said, "he probably will."

The Master of the Mint led them across to cupboards and benches, at the further side of the hall. He spoke loudly, over the noise of the machines, and the clink and snap of cut metal. On one of the benches, fashioned from steel, ball-bearings swung on the wires of an armillary sphere.

"That's interesting." The White Crow, her voice carefully neutral, peered into the armillary sphere's interstices. "This is unfinished."

"No, madam. Complete."

She touched a fingertip to the bands marking the degrees of ascension and declension. "No engravings for which Sphere each world belongs to—Hermes, Aphrodite, Kronos, or the rest."

"No, madam, and do you know why? Because it needs them not." He straightened, hands clasped behind his back in a swirl of brown satin. "You need nothing else, *nothing else* to account for the procession of worlds about the earth but the knowledge of gravitational forces! Look you, madam, you and that fool Astrologer-Royal doubtless say, with orthodoxy, that it is the planetary *numina*, the Intelligences of each Sphere, that propel the worlds in their orbits? That the *sphaera barbarica* and the paranatellons each have influence on our bodies and our fates?"

She nodded gravely.

"*Non astrum melius, sed ingenium melius*: it is not a better star which creates the genius, it is the loftier mind! The fixed stars, in their orbits a little beyond the orb of Saturn, and the sun and moon, follow a plain gravitational orbit about the earth. Nothing else but that moves them."

He waved his hand triumphantly.

"I can prove my accuracy. Look, look here." He pulled open a drawer stuffed with papers. Crabbed mathematical symbols covered every inch. "The manuscript of my *Principia Mathematica*—which the Astrologer-Royal refuses to license for publication."

She stood with her thumb hooked into her breeches belt. The long coat hung from her narrow shoulders, hem sweeping the parquet flooring. Her head turned, seeking the small boy who stood absorbed before another of the stamping-presses.

"You'd reduce the universe to a machine, Master Isaac, all springs and motion, unable to deviate, unable to change itself—and, by the by, the *earth* circles the sun."

"My observations tell me otherwise, madam. I cannot comprehend why the Astrologer-Royal perceives the world differently."

His shoulders slumped. Closing the drawer and tucking in a corner of the manuscript, he sighed.

"The universe is not animistic nor animate. Worlds do not turn because the Music of it pleases them. Weights and pulleys, madam. Wires and fulcrums. The universe can be accounted for solely on this principle."

A flurry of snow beat against the far windows. Distant, through the glass, sounded the cry of the weathervane. The White Crow raised fingertips to the feathers growing soft at her temples, and the man's gaze went past her deliberately unfocussed. One of his stubby fingers poked the air, delineating an example: "If an apple falls from a tree it strikes the earth, it can never do anything else!"

Her fingers smelled of summer apples. "I think it some while since you were in an orchard, Master Isaac."

"I have my duties here," he said regretfully, "and thus haven't time for all the observations I need. I do a little practical alchemy, also, you understand, in the furnaces . . . The salary of Master is not great. Now General Olivia wants the coinage reissued, we having suffered so greatly from counterfeiters in the late civil revolt, that I have hardly an hour to myself. Upon my retirement, I shall complete the *Principia*."

The White Crow reached into the breast of her coat. She held out a folded paper, sealed with heavy black wax.

He stared. "That's the Protector-General's seal."

"Jared, ask the gentleman at the far bench to explain the milling process to you." She lowered her voice to the decibel-level of the Mint's machinery. "Master Isaac, I didn't come to make your life easier. I came to bring the General's commission, which I like—about as much as you do. I have a carriage outside. Can your people bring it into the yards, please, and load the coin secretly as ballast?"

Cranes and gantries jutted, the tops of the tallest lost in falling snow. Snow pasted each stone, each rope, each beam; stark white against the yellow sky. Humility Talbot picked his way across a tarpaulin-shrouded stretch of earth, narrowly avoiding a ditch. His square-toed black shoes skidded. White damp-stains began to rime the worn leather uppers.

"This way, master architect."

The Lord-Architect Casaubon clutched the handle of his black umbrella with gloved hands. Fat white flakes plopped against the taut cloth, sliding wetly down to merge with the snow covering the building site. He hunched his chins down into his buttoned-up frock-coat. "You're damned close to the river."

"We have the foundations sunk well enough," Humility Talbot protested. "The whole plan is aligned according to the sacred geometries of the site."

Ponderously, the Lord-Architect folded his umbrella, shook it, handed it to Talbot to hold, and ducked under a low scaffolding platform. He pushed six inches of piled snow from the stone of the walls. It fell heavily and wetly into the dug pits of the piers and pylons. He tapped the stone.

"Master architect?"

"You're building the eye of the sun, rot it, not some village hall!"

The Lord-Architect Casaubon took one foot from an ice-starred mud slick; rubbed the upper of one of his shoes against his calf, smearing the black silk stockings; and cast another glance upwards. A lowering grey-yellow covered the vast site: stones, half-built walls, piles of uncut masonry, scaffolding, and gantries. Flakes of snow drifted down, black against the sky, white against the earth. A cold, damp wind cut through clothing.

"Where was your last trouble?"

"This way, sir."

Humility bowed his cropped head. A snatch of wind threatened to remove his wide-brimmed hat, and he crammed it down more firmly. Two braziers burned to the north, half a street down towards the river, and men clustered around them, occasionally sparing a look and a curse. He led the fat man across laid-down planks, threading a way between barrows, casks, and temporary shelters; between two towering stone walls that would in time become a perpendicular door arch.

Unroofed, a vast circular building lay open to the winter sky.

No snow lay here. Rising walls, pillars, entrance-arches, pavements: all clear. Biscuit-coloured stone took the snow's light, transmuting it to warmth, glowing back with the heat of long summers.

"Rot you, at least you have *something* right."

The Lord-Architect squatted down with slow and immense effort until he balanced on huge haunches. Without looking up, he snapped fat fingers at Humility Talbot. The Protectorate architect handed down the furled umbrella. Casaubon poked cautiously at the warm stone with the ferrule.

The gentle curve of the walls stretched away to either

side, the nearest section already lined with fluted pillars. Paving ringed the interior: a warm yellow-brown stone, inset at every heptagonal junction with a star of gold or bronze.

Between the Lord-Architect's feet, an inset oval of silver gleamed in the paving.

Just a little further in, two more curved to pattern each other; then five, seven, seventeen, and more. Glass, backed with steel and silver; thick and curved and polished to mirror-brightness, stretching out in the same pattern all around the circular building: stone pavement becoming mirror.

Three yards further in to the centre of the roofless building, the patches merged to become a plain of mirror. It gleamed, catching all light into itself, light of dull clouds, hidden sun, falling ice-flakes; glowing with a burnished silver on the verge of becoming gold.

The Lord-Architect leaned forward, pressing the umbrella ferrule into the fretwork of pale stone. The steel, smooth as mercury, reflected his black brocade sleeve.

"We laid this first, to build around it. Geomancy left us no other choice," Humility Talbot murmured. "The smaller buildings around are planned to Golden Rectangles; this to a circle, and the whole thing in just line and proportion."

The Lord-Architect planted the umbrella firmly and pushed himself upright. The umbrella's narwhal-bone ribs bent. "The dome?"

"There we had problems before . . . this . . . began. Sir, you know how it is with master masons. They have their craft, and for building square, none better, but when it comes to the structural dynamics of a dome—the weight-bearing calculations, the necessity to lay curved stone, the placing of the ribs—they must and will learn to obey orders without my explaining every reason for it!"

"Any of 'em still working here with you?"

"Yes, sir, some."

"Damn 'em for fools, then!"

Without waiting for guidance, the Lord-Architect began to pace around the pavement, staying back from the mirrored interior. Once he paused, squinting up to where the future dome would have masonry gaps to allow in the light of the sun: dawn and dusk's warm illuminations, noon's blaze.

"We prepared the ground! When there were accidents, we blessed the stones!" Humility Talbot waved his arms. "The Protector herself came here with chrism to anoint the support armature of the dome! It made no difference, sir, the walls still crack and fall when we build higher than this, and workmen are still found dead—crushed under stones, or fallen from secure scaffolding, or—and there's this."

Sound muffled: quiet enough now to hear the faint hiss of flakes melting as they fall to land on the eye of the sun. Quiet enough to hear the echoes of Humility Talbot's shouting, and his harsh breath.

The Lord-Architect placed fingertips against the inner surface of the wall. He stripped both black silk gloves off and rested his palms against the stone. A frown creased his broad forehead.

"I—ees*hou*!" The fat man blinked at the unexpected sneeze, stepped back, and wiped his nose on his sleeve. "I find this place remarkably cold, Master Talbot."

"I know. And I know that it should not be so: not the eye of the sun." Almost humbly, Talbot touched the large man's arm. "You will not say what the godless say in this town: that only the monarch could build this temple, and not we of the Protectorate?"

The Lord-Architect Casaubon stared intently at the blank wall. He frowned, the tip of his tongue protruding between his delicate lips.

"Master architect?—Ecch!"

Humility Talbot's nostrils flared whitely. He stepped back, muffling an oath.

In the almost-heat of the temple's interior, a smell grew to prominence. Coppery, cold; a taste of metal in the back of the throat. Given a wind from the river, the stench of the Smithfield shambles might be drifting up. The snow fell in soft verticals, denying the possibility, intensifying the stink of blood.

"How can I build a dome?" Talbot's voice sounded thick
with unshed tears. Plaintive, he wailed. "The stones themselves are become an abomination!"

Thick redness bulged from between the impossibly tight
masonry joins, liquefied, and ran down the sand-coloured
walls in streaks. Blood poured, running from between the
stones, dripping, spouting; until the great curving wall ran
red from top to bottom, for the space of perhaps twenty
yards either side of where they stood.

"As to th—*assshuu!*"

The Lord-Architect blew his nose between his fingers,
wiped his hand down his coat, and looked at the spreading
pool of blood as it crept across the paving towards his heeled
shoes.

A yard short of the first inset mirrors, it ceased, rapidly
coagulating to a brown scum.

"As to *that*," the Lord-Architect Casaubon concluded, "you
have me, Master Talbot, whom you did not have before."

Humility Talbot shivered. He tucked his hands into his
sleeves, thin arms shuddering at the touch of cold flesh.
"That's all very well, sir, but what do you propose to do? I
cannot return to the Protector with no reason for the temple's defilement!"

The fat man squinted bareheaded at the sky, from here
fringed with the half-built walls of the eye of the sun. His gaze
took the direct line that sunlight would take, when striking in
through the dome's empty centre to the mirror-floor.

"Cheer up, man!" His ham-sized hand landed on Humility
Talbot's shoulder. The impact staggered the smaller man.
Guileless blue eyes gazed down. "I need the hour of noon,
and a sky clear enough to see the sun; *then* I'll do a he-
liomantic diagnosis for you. Here, on this very site! Tomorrow. Why not? Then we'll see. Tell your General Olivia to
come."

He beamed in satisfaction.

Humility Talbot opened his mouth, and thought better of it.

"All things are made known in their proper time," he concluded weakly.

"Of course! Good man." The Lord-Architect nodded in a congratulatory manner. "Nothing to be done until tomorrow noon. I'm—ee*shuu*!—I'm returning to Roseveare House. Send a carriage for me there. Pray to the Universal Architect for an end to this pox-rotten snow!"

Sometime in the early hours of the next morning the Lord-Architect Casaubon wakes, turning in the creaking bed with infinite caution, so as not to wake the woman beside him. The midnight feed was long, Jadis fractious.

He rises, treading delicately towards bassinet and bottle for the next feed. Fire's embers do not take the chill from the room. He bends ponderously over to poke the child in its belly with a fat, ink-marked finger.

"Coo," he offers. "Coo?"

Wrinkled red flesh moves. A tiny and baleful pair of blue eyes opens. The Lord-Architect's three-month-old daughter, in total silence, gives him a look of withering contempt. He bundles the child in his voluminous silk robe and feeds her.

"Ookums," Casaubon tries, scooping the baby up against his vast shoulder, mildly reassured as she throws up a dribble of milk onto his lapel. "Babba . . ."

The ginger-haired child closes her eyes in what appears to be long-suffering, patient resignation.

From the bed the White Crow mutters, asleep.

Casaubon, listening, hears amid her unintelligible speech the words *Guillaime* and *Desire*.

VI

The morning smelled of chill, of the brazier-fires of chestnut sellers further down White-hall. The sedan chair thumped down into the snow outside the entrance to the Banqueting Hall. The White Crow caught up the hem of her dress with one hand, tossing a half-groat to the lead carrier with the other.

"I won't be long. Wait for me." She nodded across the street. "Be in *The New-Founde Land Arms.*"

Wind blew keen from a blue sky. Smoke rose from all the palace's cluttered chimneys. Sound carried across snow from the furthest yard. Tottering in heeled ankle boots and curs-ing yards of brocade skirt, she bundled her cloak about her and pushed her way through the crowds on the steps.

"Public audience!" a red-faced Protectorate sergeant snarled. "Get to the back of the queue!"

The White Crow shook unfamiliar unbound hair back from her face. Men and women in rags crowded the lobby and the stairs leading up from it, forcing the main door open, their breath white on the air. She looked in wonder at scabbed faces, ulcerous hands and legs, cataracted eyes.

"God save her. The Queen and her Hangman!" A man sat, crutches under his arm, withered legs sprawling.

A mess of trodden slush made the tiled floor treacherous. She stared from the doorway, over their heads, and caught the eye of the courtier in peach satin who descended the stairs, scented kerchief held to his nose. His yellow periwig something disarranged, his rouge smeared; and with a woman clinging to his arm, her dove silk dress slipping to uncover a breast, recovered with giggles.

"Waldegrave . . . ?" She shrugged and called. "Sir Denzil Waldegrave!"

The middle-aged man snapped his fingers. Two younger courtiers cleared a path between the queues of halt and sick. The White Crow opened her mouth to say *Master-Physician*, shut it again, and clacked across the tiles, skirt and cloak still held up out of the slush.

"Roseveare." The man's round face beamed, under his golden wig. He did not introduce his companion. "Madam, the Roseveare family face is unmistakable! You must be Mistress Valentine."

"*You* used to visit my father. I remember you and—your brother, was it?—at Roseveare, when I was very small. Sir Denzil, I need to see her Majesty, Carola."

He tapped his amber cane thoughtfully on the wet tiles, frowning in concentration. A susurrous of voices came from the stairs and the Banqueting Hall above.

"Today?"

"Now." She shook back folds of the satin cloak and brocade dress; the ice-blue and silver shining in the dim lobby. "Are you a good subject of the Queen, Sir Denzil?"

"Madam!"

"And easy to provoke, too." She smiled. "Well, I am more circumspect, but equally as good a subject, and I need to see Carola today. How difficult will that be?"

Denzil Waldegrave's gaze travelled across the lobby. "Most of these will find themselves turned away. She tires. Come up with me now, Mistress Valentine."

He turned a satin-and-sashed back, walking languidly up the turns of the stairs, his arm around the whore's waist;

below the shabby panelled walls and the pale patches where
oil-paintings might once have hung. The curls of his yellow
wig bobbed to his waist.

In sudden curiosity, the White Crow called, "Do you
know a captain called Pollexfen Calmady?"

"That pirate?" Waldegrave shuddered. "The man is nothing but a footpad. A *mercenary!* Were any of the family left,
they would disown him; howbeit, he had the fortune to be
left sole heir, before he gambled the estate away. I hope
you're not well-acquainted with him, madam?"

Without waiting for an answer, the round-faced man gestured the whore away, turned his head, and put his finger
to his lips.

"These Protectorate guards, madam, are more for Queen
Carola's protection than her imprisonment, you must understand. There are so many malcontents since civil revolt became amnesty."

Four black armoured musketmen lined the entrance to
the Banqueting Hall. The White Crow caught the gaze of their
hard-faced sergeant. She smoothed her brocade stomacher and
busied herself arranging the lace at her décolletage.

"—another Royalist bitch—"

Denzil Waldegrave's complexion reddened. The White
Crow smiled and rested her arm on his peach-satin sleeve.
As if it were easy, she maneuvered past the queueing sick
and into the Hall.

Snow-light gleamed in from the long rows of windows
onto the parquet flooring, bringing colour from the velvet
and brocade hangings. She stared down the vast hall. Ushers
with tall staves pushed the ragged men and women into
line. Somewhere a baby cried. She caught the gaze of a boy
with a bulbous growth at the side of his mouth, then the
crowd hid him.

"Carola still touches for the Kings' Evil." She marvelled.

"It behooves her, madam, to go cap in hand to the mob
and perform whatever they ask."

Surprised equally at shrewdness and bitterness, she glanced at Waldegrave.

"They *do* love her, madam. As they never did and never will love the soldier-whore Olivia. Come."

Light from the great square-paned windows dazzled. She stumbled, treading on the hem of her brocade gown; her hands that plucked at it hot now, and moist. Above, in gem-colours obscured by the smoke of torch-lit banquets, the Reubens ceiling glowed. She lowered her head from images of planetary *numina* in all glory to the purple canopy of the throne, from which focal point alone they would appear in perfect perspective, and to the woman who lolled back in it, swarthy face grinning.

"Valentine? Mistress, you've long been absent from our court. We should be greatly angered with you."

The White Crow curtsied unsteadily. The large woman in green silk and silver lace leaned forward under the throne's jewel-embroidered canopy. One of the courtiers in the lobby now stood at Carola's side, smugly informative. The White Crow wobbled upright, kicking a yard of skirt out of the way with her heel, and approached as the Queen indicated. "Your Majesty."

An old woman on her knees before the throne turned her head, showing an ulcerated mouth. Green-and-yellow pus made one cheek puffy. Rheumy eyes glared at the White Crow.

The swarthy Queen raised her voice.

"We will end what we have begun here, madam Valentine, before we speak with you. Nothing else becomes our majesty but to care for our people."

"Even so, your Majesty." Urbane, the White Crow bowed her head and retreated a step to stand beside Sir Denzil Waldegrave. He nodded fractionally in approval.

Footsteps and voices echoed down the oblong hall. Light fell on ragged cotton shirts and leather breeches, on thin and famine-worn faces.

The White Crow let her gaze travel around—rouged and beauty-marked men in red and gold silk watching an impromptu theatre performance at one window; an old woman in jade silks, a boy no older than Bevil dancing attendance on her; groups at tables gambling with cards and dice. Their groomed wigs askew, two men with rouged cheeks handled a young woman with the clean face of a whore. Ragged children ran through the crowded court, selling winter's delicacies: fried hedgepig, roast rook.

"Now, old grandmother." Queen Carola reached out, sallow fingers touching the old woman's face. Spots of dried blood marked her bitten-down nails. The stench of unwashed linen drifted from the old woman, and a whiff of rot touched the chill air.

Carola wiped her hand hard across the old woman's mouth, smearing yellow pus. The kneeling woman swayed. Carola muttered, inaudible. She pushed her hand back. "There."

The old woman slowly dabbed the smeared pus away with her sleeve. Under it, her skin showed, wrinkled and spotted brown with age. Her searching fingers touched the ulcers that had edged her lips—dry, healing scars.

"Oh, lady, bless you!"

Carola sprawled back, nodding. "Well, madam grandmother. It is well."

"*—all blessings on you—!*"

"Help her, sir." One languid hand gestured to a courtier, who took hold of the old woman's arm, helping her away. The Queen wiped her stained fingers on her rich silk breeches.

"We have need of refreshment. Our people will not grudge an hour?"

Raucous public reassurance echoed in the Banqueting Hall. Carola stood and picked up her long cane, snapping her fingers. Four or five spaniels in ruby-studded collars sprang up and tumbled about her feet as she walked towards the antechamber door.

"Valentine."

"Your Majesty."

"Waldegrave, see we are not disturbed." The door clicked shut, cutting off sound.

The swarthy woman stopped facing the window, staring down at the morning and the frozen Thamys. Black curls fell to the small of her back, dark against the green silk of her coat and knee-breeches. She turned, one hand tugging the lace at her throat.

"How long is it since *The Masque of Death and Diamonds?*"

Black eyes glinted, humourously. She reached for the chocolate Nipples of Venus that stood on a plate on a side-table, cramming one into her mouth.

"Damnation, is it *twenty* years?"

"Close on, your Majesty."

"And you had the temerity to leave our court. Or was it tact?"

The White Crow folded her cloak and put it over the back of a chair. This small, furniture-cluttered chamber boasted a fire, and she stretched out her hands to the heat.

"Tact." She shrugged one bare, chilled shoulder. "I've come to collect on the debt, your Majesty."

"Indeed? You're not the only one to use the amnesty to attempt that." The woman laughed, a resonant richness. "We gave them the answer that we'll give you—although we give it to you with less excuse. It is none the less true. Despite all you see here, the royal treasury is *bare*. Bare as Olivia's heart."

The last words came with lazy precision, as if presented on a stage. The White Crow cocked her head at the panelled walls, raising an eyebrow. The Queen crossed to a small door, flung it open, and jerked her head at the muscular dark boy sprawling on a bed in the room. He sulkily rose and walked towards the exit. Carola ran a hand over his tightly clothed buttocks as he passed.

"Now we're not overheard."

The White Crow watched a reflection in the window, overlaying the frozen river and the north bank. A woman in a blue, lace-decorated gown, hair tumbling loose; nothing of the Scholar-Soldier or Master-Physician about her. "The scars?"

The older woman pushed heavy ringlets away from her temples. The faintest white scars marked her skin. "We remember. You were only a child. Your eyes so huge . . . you looked up from the pavane and cried *'Ware candle, your hair's afire!'* And muffled us in your gown when no one dared touch the royal person before she burned into disfigurement."

"I remember."

"We would have recognised you without spies to tell us."

The White Crow stepped forward and took a wine-glass from another table. "The Queen and her Hangman."

She drank.

Wine tanged in her mouth, cold and numbing. Carola sprawled down on the couch, tossing wine-soaked biscuits to the spaniels. The White Crow walked unsteadily over and sat down on the same couch, in a swathe of brocade. *"Now—"*

The swarthy woman stared at her in glacial outrage.

"If you cannot show respect, we can ban you the commonwealth!"

"I am not used to monarchs. Nor to this land. It ought to have been my home and it never was." The White Crow looked up with eyes clear as cold water. "Listen to me while I collect on the debt you owe me. I have six thousand guineas. *Take it.* I have it: it's all I can do."

"All? We expect more loyalty from one of the ancient houses."

Half-humourous, half-despairing, her gaze met Carola's.

"When I left this was still one commonwealth. No civil revolt, no war . . . it didn't matter then if Roseveare's sympathies were Puritan or Catholic. Your Majesty, for the sake of childhood, when just seeing the court in procession used to make my heart turn over with pride, I come to you with what little help I can give. And—because of what I've seen since, people leeched to death to keep your court in toys and luxuries—this is all the help I can or will ever give."

The woman opened lazy eyes, looking up through black curls, and snapped, "Stand *up.* Now. Yes."

Unsteady, knees rubbery, the White Crow stood.

"There is a window through there." One nail-bitten hand gestured towards the Banqueting Hall. "One January day they built a scaffold outside it, and my father walked through, and they cut off his head upon a block. His own people! For whose government his nature was too mild, too gentle, too honest and civil. I saw Roseveare in the crowd! Saints became serpents, and doves became devils . . . Do you think I will take anything from traitors?"

The White Crow sighed. "I was out of the commonwealth, then, your Majesty. Far from here. And that is not all the truth about your father."

A spaniel whined. Carola rubbed its head absently. She leaned back, a large woman of some presence, staring out from under black brows. One heeled and buckled shoe tapped the carpet.

"If you owe me any debt, pay it by taking Roseveare's gift. My duty to your Majesty." The White Crow's hands fisted. Her lungs a hot void, she drew shallow breath. "As for what use you put it to—to raise troops, to corrupt whores, feast, found an art gallery, go into exile, put another bridge across the Thamys—*I don't care.*"

The White Crow stood motionless, aware of the faint voices beyond the door and the crackling of the fire. The purity of the morning sky burned beyond frost-patterned glass. She put the wine-glass down, releasing it from whitened fingers; and drew a deep breath. The scent of dogs and upholstery filled her nostrils.

Carola sighed. "You have returned no honest soul, I think."

"Honest enough. No monarchist."

"Olivia's woman, then?"

"That neither."

The White Crow picked up her flowing dress, hooked one foot behind the other, and sank into a curtsey. She backed to the door. As it opened, the black-ringleted woman's resonant voice sounded again:

"Roseveare, of *course* we'll take your money. Who'd be

such a fool as to refuse six thousand guineas? But don't show
your face in our court again. We consider we pay all debts,
tolerating your outburst. We tell you where you stand now."

The swarthy woman held up her bitten, ringed hand;
thumb and forefinger a fraction apart.

"*This* close to Newgate prison."

The sun hung high in the south. Blue-and-rose shadows
clung to the curves of fallen snow. Olivia trod down the
crispness. She raised her head, stopping abruptly amid the
crowd of aides and captains.

"Is it noon yet?"

Dozens of soldiers crowded the trenches, half-built walls,
masonry piles, and snow-shrouded gantries of the site. Sun
glinted from mail, black armour, and faces reddened by the
cold. Massed breath steamed up into the air. Talk quietened
as she strode past.

"The bell in Ludgate struck quarter-to, madam General,
no great while since."

"Good Master Cord, find me the architect."

Cord-of-Discipline Mercer floundered across a hollow,
where snow had drifted in the night. The young man vanished into the crowd at the foot of the nearest crane. Olivia
spared a glance up at counterweight and pulley and gantry,
their iron-cuffed wood bright against a blue sky.

Her eyes narrowed.

"Tell Master Cord he may save his labour." She pitched
her voice to carry. "*Architect Casaubon!*"

The great wooden platform built for lifting masonry rocked
in the freezing air. Chains and ropes groaned. The man
inside raised one fat arm, signalling, and the crane pivoted
slowly. Olivia gazed up at the vast figure of the Lord-Architect on the platform.

"Good day to you, madam!"

His booming voice rang out across the eye of the sun,
succeeded by a whisper. Crammed in a corner of the platform, somewhat green, and in shadow, a crop-haired man

stood with both hands locked about the wooden rail. "Madam Protector . . ."

"Master Humility," she acknowledged cheerfully. "How are your consultations, master? What conclusion have you arrived at?"

She signalled. The platform lowered, settling on packed snow some ten yards outside the circular walls. She barely glanced at that sandstone-brightness, uncanny in the white landscape.

"I've shown Master Casaubon where we attempted to build the support armature for the dome. And over what area the destroyed beams were found." Humility Talbot's white and gloveless hands gripped the rail. "He advises, Protector, that no human foot be set upon the stone while this attempt is made to discover causes."

"I see."

She snapped her fingers. Humility Talbot scrambled from the basket, stumbling on solid earth and snow, red to the ears and panting. His eyes shifted wildly. Olivia cast an eye up at the crane.

"Mistress Patience, help me unbuckle this breastplate. Lend me your cloak, Master Talbot."

Freed of weight, she swung the cloak about her shoulders, fastened the clasp, and swung over the rail and into the masonry platform. Icy wind blew, briefly, in her yellow-grey hair, moving the wispy curls across her eyes. She rubbed her nose with a leather-gauntleted hand.

"I understand that the sighting itself will be done from here? Very well, master architect. I accompany you."

The Lord-Architect blinked at her from slightly red-rimmed eyes. He sniffed, cavernously; beaming; rolls of fat creasing his cheeks. "Most welcome!"

Sun glittered here and there on the heads of crossbow-bolts, on basket-hilted swords, and long pikes. The planks jerked under her boots. She grinned, fiercely, the cold freezing her lips, and busied herself with wrapping her muffler more firmly about her neck as the platform lifted into the air.

"Now, sir, you are the safest you have ever been."
Amused, Olivia leaned her arms on the railing, staring
down. "Since I believe all these within my sight, at least,
are loyal. And now we may speak together privately."

Rising, the wooden scaffolding platform creaked alarming-
ly, seventy feet above the earth.

"Master architect?"

"A calculated strain." The Lord-Architect waved his fat
hand casually. "High eno—*ee*shou!"

The plank platform twisted gently. The Lord-Architect
Casaubon wiped his nose on his sleeve, leaving a wet silver
trail across the black brocade. He squinted up at the noon
sun. "High enough."

She raised a gloved hand, waving to the man, just visible,
in the crane's cabin. The counterbalanced gantry swung with
a gradual speed. The platform moved smoothly, earth sliding
away beneath, replaced by stone, until it hung directly over
the circular wall of the eye of the sun.

"Just so high will the golden sphere stand, that I will have
placed on the dome." Her warm breath moistened the wool
muffler. She tugged it down, rubbing at her bulbous nose
and cheeks, and stretched her shoulders; cold's rheumatism
fading in the glory of height and clarity.

Below, the site spread out, the geometry of circles and
rectangles plainly visible under the snow. Groups of workmen clustered around braziers and toolhuts, their pencil-
shadows short and north-pointing. Beyond them the land
sloped down through two streets to the river, an expanse of
frozen white. General Olivia stared first across the Thamys
at the far shore of Northbankside, and the distant hills of
Middlesex and Rutland.

"An old city, master architect."

She turned, facing south now, the noon sun almost warm
on her skin. She laughed, small and gruff, dazzled. To east
and south and west, snow-covered gambrel roofs, spires,
crenellated towers, warehouses, palaces. Smoke threaded up
from chimneys. A rook winged lazily northwards towards the

river. Olivia gripped the rail in one hand, leaning out. Beyond the soldiers and masons, people crowded well-trodden paths about Smithfield and Spitalfields and the city-wall gates; riders and carriages coming in towards the markets, a bonfire burning down towards the convent garden.

"You would not know, from here, that all totters again on the edge of civil revolt. Amnesty is a fragile plant, easily blasted. I have said we puritans are the heirs of the pagan Romans, who by their Mithras foreshadowed our Lord. Is that true, master architect, do you think?"

"Oh, indubitably." The Lord-Architect took out an off-white kerchief, brandishing it. He leaned over the side of the platform and waved expansively to the crowd below. "Cooee!"

Faintly, a few answering catcalls drifted up. The large man beamed.

He swung his arm in a half-circle. Olivia ducked easily and came up again. His pudgy finger ticked off the panorama of Whitehall Palace, Observatory and Mint, the Guildhall; all the great facades lining frozen Thamys: "Fantastic carapaces!"

"Sir?"

Stray wind blew his cropped copper-red hair across his forehead. He shoved clumsily at it with a half-gloved hand, eyes squinting against the brightness and void of air, and clapped her on the back.

"Buildings—our fantastic carapaces of the soul! Vitruvius writes that all habitations, laid out according to line and true proportion, reflect the lineaments of the universe itself . . ." His eyes opened wider, a startling bright blue; lost in a delight of theory. "Like caddis-fly cases, cities *grow*."

"Over many generations." She stared down. "This town has stood against war and famine, kept by plain men and women who suffered monarchy until it grew tyrannous. And who will not suffer it now. Yet I do wonder. I do wonder, master architect, whether the blood-royal that has nourished the buildings of this city be necessary still."

Foundations and outlines of towers, nave, and courtyards

rumpled the site's covering snow. She stared down. Directly beneath, across a void of chill air, naked stone shone. Warm, startlingly delicate white stone shown now by contrast with the snow to be biscuit-coloured. The foundation, piers, and pylons of the dome.

Baroque, fretted, bright as the noon sun itself, the inlaid mirror of the central hall shone.

"*Sol invictus!*" She crossed herself devoutly.

From here, the separate inlays formed a pattern: clusters of tiny particles that became larger, baroque shapes that, seen from a proper perspective, formed feathered eyes, stylised wings, all facing inward to where inlaid steel and silver merged in one blaze of light.

"There!" Triumphant, she grabbed his coat-sleeve. "Look you there, master architect!"

Hanging above a circle of mirror, pure as cold Western lakes, she stared down into reflection. A fringe of inward-leaning stone walls: perpendicular arches and half-windows. The underside of the minuscule plank-platform. Even the dots of their white faces. And held within that stone foil, lambent as sapphires—the azure winter sky.

The cold air smelled slaughterhouse-warm, rich suddenly with blood. Thinned oxygen whispered in her lungs.

Bulging up from beneath, coiling masses of guts pressed against the mirror. Flesh roiled. Bloody lights, torn muscle, ropes of entrails and bowel: blue and purple and red: all Smithfield's abattoirs, all the Thamys's shambles, all the battlefields of the civil revolt could not fill the Pit so disclosed. Demon faces formed and dissolved.

She coughed, wiping streaming eyes.

"Be certain I have not lacked, neither, for those who attribute disasters here either to ill-luck, or the Lord's will. It is otherwise."

The stench abated.

"Demonic manifestations, eh? You should have called me in the sooner." The Lord-Architect wrested one of the ornate rings from his fat fingers and sprang it open with a nail to disclose, as it unfolded, a miniature armillary sphere. He clicked the bevel of another ring, which lifted to show the spike of a miniature sundial; busying himself between the two for some moments.

"Noon in thirty heartbeats."

Both rings clicked shut and were returned to their respective fingers. The fat man removed a notebook from his coat-tail pocket. His breath misted the air around his face. Drops of sweat slid down his face, runnelling over chins into a wilting lace cravat. He fumbled in the pockets of his tightly buttoned black frieze coat.

The Protector-General flattened herself back against the rail as he turned around, buffeted by elbow and buttock. "I rely on you, sir. To tell me answers that, for all their expertise, my plain men do not dare tell me."

The Lord-Architect extracted a pencil and held it up in brief triumph.

"Sir—"

"Rot it, be *quiet*, can't you? Heliomancy takes concentration."

Amused, cold, dizzy with the exhilaration of height, she smiled and leaned back, her arms outstretched along the platform's rails. A smell of sand and earth clung to the wood.

The fat man looked south.

Following his gaze for the briefest second, her eyes filled with the sun's blazing whiteness. She muttered a curse. Green-and-purple images swum in her vision, blotting out the snow-covered cityscape below and the purity of blue sky.

"Master architect?"

"*Hurts*, rot it."

Faint freckles stood out on his pale skin. The delicately carved lips thinned. His head lowered and she stared through blotched sight into blinded, dazzled blue eyes. One half-gloved hand fumbled pencil and notebook, and the fat man sketched, with quick and fine accuracy, the shapes of the images swimming behind eyelids.

"There!" He snapped the book shut, beaming. "You're fortunate to have me, madam. Any other architect would take a week to draw up these configurations. Send a carriage for me and I'll bring the answers along tomorrow."

The White Crow pulled the nursery door closed, listened in the hall for a moment to Jared's quiet breathing, and plodded downstairs to the kitchens. An ache born of snowwalking burned in her calves.

"And to think I sometimes wish I was back on the road." The White Crow grinned at Abiathar. "The life of a Scholar-Soldier was always better indoors; don't let me tell you any different!"

The older woman chuckled, handing over a mug of mulled wine. The White Crow slumped in the kitchen chair, the warmth of ovens blasting against her skin; sighed, and slid down so that she drank from the mug at a dangerous angle, a few drops spilling onto her shirt.

"The little one's asleep."

"Good . . . did she take her bottle well?"

"Sweet as a nut." Abiathar's tone chilled. "How you can think of risking yourself at the court, and that baby depending on you, *I* don't know."

Hanging hams, sausages; new loaves wrapped in cloth; jars of preserves and heavy iron pans: all blurred in her sight with a sudden rush of sleep. The White Crow blinked gritty eyes. "If I don't sort this out, it's flee the commonwealth, and Jared and the baby with me. The which I would prefer to be a little older, before I travel again."

The White Crow looked over the rim of her pewter mug. Spices and red wine stained her mouth. She licked her lips.

The older woman wiped her hands on a kitchen cloth. "As if you hadn't been fretting to travel since the day you came back to Roseveare!"

"Me? No. I don't carry sword-and-pack now . . . Am I a disappointment to you all?"

Abiathar shrugged plump shoulders. "Ask Hazelrigg or Kitterage when they come in. Tell me the truth. How long before you leave us again?"

"Roseveare ought to have a different heir. Jared would—
no, he wouldn't," the White Crow concluded. "He'd live
here in town, and be a merchant on the 'Change. At least
I'm as confused by that boy as Roseveare ever was by me."

"And now we sit here with half a king's fortune in the
coach-house—"

"Oh, what?" The White Crow sat up. She banged the
pewter mug down on the scrubbed kitchen table. "That's
from my having Kitterage drive the coach, I suppose? If he
can't keep his mouth shut outside the house we'll all have
more trouble than we know what to do with . . ."

"Speaking of trouble." Abiathar grunted. She reached up
to the shelf over the range. "There's a message left for you."

The White Crow unfolded the scrap of paper.

*Madam i hope this findes you in good health. I desire
you will examine me as you promis'd you should, for
dis-ease or else for whether i am carrying an unlawfull
child. Yr servant in the Lord. Guillaime*

"Yes . . . I did promise her that."

"Dirty soldier's whore!"

"Roseveare owes her!"

The White Crow stood, stretched, and walked out of the
kitchen, rapidly climbing narrow stairs; three flights and
then four, slowing as she reached the living rooms at the
top of the house.

Deep voices resonated down the stairwell.

A sudden recognisable burst of laughter made her stop,
frown, and walk on up more slowly. The door banged open
as she reached for the handle.

"Dress, little one! Prepare! Tonight is the night of—*asshuu!*"

The Lord-Architect Casaubon searched in two pockets,
and unearthed from his buttoned-back cuff an immense
brown handkerchief. He wiped his nose.

"Of the Astrologers' Feast, yes." The White Crow stood
on her toes, attempting to see past the fat man and into the

room. "I have every intention of being there, given an hour to rest beforehand—*Casa*ubon!"

The Lord-Architect stepped out. She walked in. Just too early for lamps; light flickered from the hearth-fire and reflected up from the torches below in Roseveare Court. Lady Arbella Lacey, Gadsbury, Bevil Calmady, and the Margrave Linebaugh glanced up from their card-playing by the bright hearth.

"Ah."

Dimness muted his scarlet brocade coat. The trailing white lace cravat stood out, that and his pale face under the darkness of the periwig's curls. The gentleman-mercenary captain Pollexfen Calmady sprawled in a winged armchair. His eyes flicked up to meet hers, with a brilliance either manic humour or ironic despair.

"Polly was arrested." The Lord-Architect waved an airy hand. "Who else could he come to for bail? I must shift my shirt before we go out—"

"*Bail?*"

The door clicked shut behind the Lord-Architect's large and rapidly departing back. The White Crow bit down on what she might have wished to shout after him. She crossed to the window and stared out.

Pollexfen Calmady's voice came ironically from the chair. "Madam, I'm your lawful guest, it appears. Indeed, the courts say I may not now avoid your hospitality without being unlawful—at least until they try me."

The White Crow breathed on the window-glass and rubbed a clearness, looking down at quiet fallen snow, trodden into a mire outside the bookshops, and the booksellers' doors thrown open and spilling yellow light.

Soundless, Pollexfen Calmady appeared by her side. His coat smelled faintly of scent and ordure. One of the wig's harsh curls scratched her cheek.

"Selling broadsheets," he said thoughtfully, "every hour of night and day, new ones."

"Don't fear. You'll have your turn in the Newgate broadsheets."

He turned, facing her in the dim room, drawing the skirts of his coat slightly back. Sword-hanger and blade both gone. He smiled crookedly. At the hearth, the card game continued.

"I appreciate that I am not a welcome guest. Nor, things standing as they do between myself and your husband, a guest that you can refuse."

He shrugged.

"And the girl is your patient, Master-Physician; yes, all this I see clearly. But see you, I did no more harm to her than any sleeping husband who wakes to find himself in congress with his wife. If she have a child, I'll pay for it— if ever I have money. And if she needs a name I'll wed her, although truth to tell, there are those yet living who have had that privilege before her."

The White Crow looked down at her hands. The faint luminosity of *magia* touched her skin, no brighter in this dim room than in full sunlight; pregnant with the possibilities of healing and destruction.

"*Excuse me.*"

She inclined her head curtly to Bevil and the rest, walking out. A few yards down the corridor she kicked a bedroom door open, walked in, shut it, and leaned back against the wood.

The Lord-Architect Casaubon stood with his shirt-sleeved arms over his head, fingers almost touching the plaster ceiling, his head muffled in the shirt's vast folds. Unbuttoned green silk breeches wrinkled massively across his buttocks and thighs. His elbows worked: muffled muttering succeeded by a ruffled crop of copper-gold hair emerging.

"Little one."

Abrupt, he reached one fat finger to stroke her cheek. The White Crow absently pulled the drawstrings at his sleeve and tied the laces in a loose bow.

"The man is a rapist," she said dangerously.

"He is one of my oldest friends."

"Whom you haven't seen for—*how* long?"

The Lord-Architect shrugged magnificently. "He came to me for help; could I refuse him?"

"You? Well, no, *you* . . ." The White Crow shook her head. "But staying in this house?"

"Terms of bail," Casaubon explained. "And in any case, little one, he had a claim on my hospitality. Blackmail."

"What?"

"If I hadn't conceded, he swore he'd tell you how I wrote to him last summer, and persuaded him to put my name to the Protectorate for the repair of the eye of the sun."

"You *wrote*—"

The White Crow opened and shut her mouth several times. In the lamplight's yellow softness, she watched the Lord-Architect tucking in his shirt and buttoning his breeches up the sides, one hand reaching over his immense shoulder to grab the trailing ends of his braces.

"Yes. I can see that you wouldn't have wanted him to tell me that."

"You'd be angry," Casaubon explained, "given that you don't know about it."

The cinnamon-haired woman choked, and rubbed moisture out of the corner of her eye with her knuckle. She seized his wrist, that her two hands together could not reach around.

"I might have guessed. I might have *known*—"

He looked down at her over the swell of chins, chest, and shoulder. "I believe I didn't quite catch that?"

"I said," the White Crow observed, "it's a good thing that he didn't tell me, and that I don't know!"

VII

The astrologer William Lilly
plodded on from Eleanor's Cross in the dusk. White snow
gleamed on the gables of the overhanging houses. He
trudged through slush trodden black, and over the yellow
stains of chamber-pots emptied from upstairs windows.

A wolf howled.

He dug his chin into his collar, head down, hurrying for
the arched entrance to St. Martin's disused wine cellars.
Torchlight and voices came up the steps: infallible signs of
the Astrologers' Feast. He hacked snow from his boots on
the worn brick steps.

A rough-coated body pushed past his legs.

"God's teeth, man!"

The wolf barged down the stairway, paws splaying, head
low. Mange marked its grey-black pelt. William Lilly abandoned the entrance-way, slush and a searing cold wind blow-
ing in, and followed. The wolf's muzzle swung to give him
one glance with eyes as pale as ice. Scars and ribs could
equally be seen under the thinning fur.

"Cannot you take a little more care?"

He came down off the last step. The arched brick vault
danced with torchlight, shadows, and smoke. Immense bar-

rels lined each side. At the far end, beyond an iron grating, the noise of the Feast's preparation echoed. Here nitre clung to the walls, and brickwork smelled of graves. The wolf whined, pawing at a heap of clothes.

Pale skin spread through its pelt.

Its bent limbs lengthened, straightened, grew. A faint cracking of bone echoed.

A shadow leaped upright on the wall.

The young man, his naked back to Lilly, and every knob of vertebrae standing sharply in relief, reached down and swung the bundle of clothes up. He thrust head and arms awkwardly through a black robe's neck and sleeves.

"Sir, I apologise." He bowed as he turned, adjusting his white falling-band and the belt of the robe. "I beg your pardon—unseemly—but my late arrival—"

William Lilly met the young priest's gaze: colourless as ice. Underfoot, sawdust clogged with wetness; the pine-smell overlaying dankness and the perfume of oil-lamps. He bent and picked up a black-covered book that had fallen from the bundle of clothes. "Yours, sir, I think."

"I thank you, yes." A shy smile. "It is the first time I will have preached at the Astrologers' Feast. I'm to give the later sermon. The text being Genesis 1:14, 'Let there be lights in the firmament of the heaven . . . and let them be for signs.' "

"Then let me be first to bid you welcome. '*Non cogunt:* the stars do not compel.' " Citing the Feast's watchword, William Lilly took the arm of the young werewolf-priest and walked on into the crowded cellars beyond.

"Master Lilly."

The White Crow shrugged her shoulders, sitting back from the piles of open books on the table. Muscles loosened and lost tension. For a moment she stared into unfocussed middle distance, not seeing around her the powdered wigs, brocade coats and black robes, and the ruddy faces of the assembly.

"Mistress White Crow."

She smiled up at the thin man. "Will you thank your compatriots again for letting me use their library here?"

Voices burred. Above forty men and women stood talking in the cellars; some here in the fire- and damp-proof library, more through in further rooms lined with old casks and heated with iron braziers. She unbuttoned her doublet, hot for the first time in days.

"May I help?"

"I'd be glad of it." She pushed at the sprawl of papers on the long bench and shifted a pile of emphemerides-tables. "Geomancy isn't my best line of work. And I'm not the architect in my family."

"I perceived Master Casaubon was unwell." The man smoothed his black gown as he seated himself on the opposite side of the table. His dark hair he wore long and natural. "I can calculate you a reading of any subject, event, or question within seven to ten minutes."

A large man in a curled grey wig and strawberry silk leaned over his shoulder. "What, Master Lilly? *Still* practising horary astrology?"

He raised his head, taking in the White Crow.

"Elias Ashmole, ma'am. Astrologer-Royal. This dunderhead still thinks he can predict an answer based upon the astrological moment of *asking the question*! Pure foolishness and delusion. If you have not the exact hour of a subject's birth, how may you predict anything?"

The White Crow leaned back and put one foot up on the bench, clasping her hands round her knee. She grinned.

"I'm by no means certain, masters, that prediction is possible in this uncertain world. The Invisible College has always denied it. Else where's free will? But it so happens that I need a reading of the Celestial Spheres, not for a person, but for a certain construction-site—"

Elias Ashmole held up a fleshy hand. "No names. Madam, I beg you, no names. Our rules at these Feasts are, no oaths to be sworn, no toasts drunk to any faction, and *no* discus-

sion of sympathies in the present civil disorder. How else
could we continue to meet in harmony?"

"Well, yes, Elias, and I am certain she knows all of that,
being a magus." William Lilly chuckled. "Nor I will not say
that I do not recognise what is this date of construction you
have here. But to the meat of the matter: what should the
analysis discover?"

"Why such a sacred site is plagued with demonic
manifestations."

"Well now . . . I'll see what I can do." His dark head
bent over the papers. "Pay me in kind: a Thamys salmon,
or a hare; a sack of coal; something of that. No one is rich
as the world stands now. Let me see . . ."

Ashmole tutted.

The White Crow settled back. Her shoulder bumped solidity. She raised her head, apologising; and a small and
wispy-haired man blinked through half-spectacles at her.

"Madam Roseveare." He smiled shyly. "Could you spare
me a little time, I wonder, for some speech about
antiquities?"

"I beg your pardon?"

Unperturbed, the man gathered his moth-eaten robes
about him and bowed.

"Your childhood recollections of Roseveare and this noble
town of ours before the civil war. Such things are of great
interest to me. I am writing a—no, I cannot call it a history,
it is too brief. A collection of the lives of those whose names
history should not forget. I wonder, madam, if you might
speak to me. Even a child's memories may be useful."

The White Crow smiled wryly. "Yes, later, Master . . ."

"Aubrey. John Aubrey, madam." He blinked and removed
his spectacles, disclosing a young face surprisingly sharp and
tenacious. "Please remember that *I* spoke with you first. My
friend Master Evelyn has a diary that he is completing, on
much inferior lines, and I wish my own work to see the
printer or ever his should."

"Yes . . ." The White Crow inclined her head. "Excuse me, sir, please."

The group of astrologers closed in around table and charts. She grunted, stretching, and walked down to the further table and slumped into the chair beside the Lord-Architect Casaubon.

"Having such a body of knowledge here it'd be criminal not to use it, but—! All this tolerance is beginning to get on my nerves. If I see one more royalist and puritan propagandist—beg pardon, 'astrological pamphleteer'—breaking bread together . . . Here's Lilly drinking with Ashmole: you wouldn't think they'd been calling each other *the Commonwealth's Exrement* in a half-dozen broadsheets this month."

Casaubon, head bent over plans, compasses, square, and rule, grunted.

"Oh . . . they may well keep in with each other, I suppose. They're going to need friends, whichever side wins. What have you got?"

Casaubon sniffed. "I am not a superstitious man. I refuse to believe hocus-pocus about the necessity for 'royal' blood! Patently obviously there is some fault in the proportions and patterns of the eye of the sun, that encourages disorder to manifest itself there. *Patently* obviously—"

He coughed cavernously. The White Crow looked at his flushed face above his unlaced shirt, noting beads of sweat that plastered his copper-red hair to his forehead.

"Except that I confess I cannot find it!"

She stood, pushing papers and books aside, and walked around him until she could lean on his shoulders, and put her arms about his neck. His fair skin burned. She rested her cheek against his, that sweat made warmly wet.

"I saw Carola touching for Kings' Evil today. It worked. She healed people. I saw."

His vast chest rose and fell, the thickness of his breathing audible. The Lord-Architect frowned.

"Blood-royal? *Eee*shou!"

She stepped back. The Lord-Architect Casaubon squinted and felt the back of his head, apparently in some surprise that it was still there. He wiped his sleeve across his face. Phelgm trailed down onto the waistcoat that barely contained his belly.

"I—*shaaa!*"

The White Crow hauled a kerchief out of her breeches pocket and thrust it at him. He took it gratefully, wiping his reddened, streaming nose. He looked up through watery eyes.

"Rot it, I *almost* know!"

"I'll keep searching." She walked over to the further shelves, elbowing between two arguing astrologers and an alchemist. Her finger traced bookspines, stopping at familiar bindings, and she hooked out a three-volume set of the *De Occulta Philosophica,* a second edition of *Ghâya,* the *Novum Organum,* and a much-thumbed *Picatrix,* and dumped them on the nearest unoccupied table.

Three minutes after she seated herself, a shadow crossed the lamplight.

"Damned ruffians! They nearly had my carriage over in Oxford Street." A small man beat snow from his black coat. Breaking off in mid-movement, he leaned across the trestle-table and spoke quite naturally: "There is a theosophist work you should read, Madam Valentine, if you haven't: *Under the Shadow of Bright Wings—*"

"*—In the Heart of the Womb,*" Valentine White Crow completed. She lowered her voice slightly. "You're the first of the College I've met here, Master . . ."

"Harvey, William Harvey. Ashmole told me you were come. Your reputation goes before you."

"And yours, sir. I know you for our foremost surgeon."

William Harvey seized a chair and turned it about, and sat with his arms resting along the back, and his chin on his arms. She judged him in his thirties; a short, neat man with hair powdered and drawn back, and brilliant dark eyes.

"Overturned carriage?" she queried, closing a book and keeping her thumb in the place. "Would that have to do with your medical research?"

He snorted with laughter without moving his chin from his arms, so that his shoulders jolted. "It would. Damn me if I didn't take *four* sword-and-dagger men to Tyburn with me this time, thinking that's enough—and we cut the man down fairly, after many had come up to take the benefit of a hanged criminal's touch on head or breast—and had him shrouded and, as I thought, on the way to the Anatomy Hall. Halfway down Oxford Street I hear a cry. *'Reverence the dead!'* So we whip up the horses, and race a mob of two hundred . . ."

He lifted his head and spat on the sawdust floor.

"You'll be pleased to know I keep the Invisible College's name somewhat distanced from this, or else *you'd* find a Tyburn riot at your door."

Conscious of the smooth movement of muscles under her skin as she stretched, feeling the blood's beat in her temples, the White Crow smiled ruefully. "You understand their fears. To be dead and buried is one thing, to be cut up under arc-lights and studied . . ."

"How else can some ruffian make restitution for a crime? This whelp had all his friends there to see him turned off, and every one of 'em determined he should be of no more use afterwards but to be packed in clay and left to rot."

Sir William Harvey spread thin, strong fingers; lamplight glinting from an onyx ring.

"I've tracked the blood's circulation, by examining where it passes through artery and vein. How else now can I examine different kinds of blood, without I have blood in profusion to do as I like with? Precious few will give it living; I have to make do with the dead."

Letting go of the third volume of *De Occulta Philosophica*, the White Crow turned her wrist over so that the back of her hand rested on the table. Her left index finger stroked the skin, leaving a faint pale-rose illumination; all the sensations of the hard bench, echoing cellar, odours of cooking and parchment, cold air and men's sweat, intensified as she measured the subliminal drumming of a pulse.

"Madam Valentine?"

"Agrippa writes that the heart's blood is under the Sign of Helios; the blood of the extremities under—?"

"Technically, Thoth or Isis, according to ascendant." Harvey leaned forward, one finger prodding the bench. "Or, as it seems to me in my discoveries this last year, the constitution of blood is as individual as the constitution of your astrological nativity. The magus Agrippa hadn't my modern advantages. I've put blood to Chemicall analysis, finding in it, for each man or woman, a *unique* combination of such Elements as Paracelsus describes."

"If that's true . . ."

Large hands cupped her shoulders from behind, the hot palms dampening the cloth of her doublet. Harvey's gaze lifted—and lifted again. She leaned back against the Lord-Architect's stomach, feeling him sway slightly, and blinked at the sudden strong odour of wintergreen and brandy.

"You heard?"

" 'Blood-royal.' The virtues of individual blood!" The Lord-Architect hit his fist into his other ham-sized hand, with a sound that echoed off the cellar's curved walls. Four or five people glanced round. He beamed at them.

"Casaubon?"

Overhanging the trestle-table, the Lord-Architect Casaubon held one hand up precariously and wiggled spread fingers.

"Pox rot it, it was there in front of me! You told me. *She bites her fingers.* Enough to cause blood to flow. And then touches for the Kings' Evil . . . And heals it, with whatever the virtue of her particular blood is. Amazing the woman isn't dead of some disease by now."

The White Crow looked up over the swell of his black satin waistcoat, and the brandy-stained lace ruffles at his chins, and met the Lord-Architect's gaze. Sweat runnelled his face. She stood up, grabbed his sleeve, pushed him into her chair, and hitched herself up to sit on the table between Casaubon and the surgeon.

"I thought you were the one who didn't believe in the mystical virtues of the blood-royal?"

Both the Lord-Architect's elbows hit the table. The White Crow winced, feeling the vibration through buttock and hip. He leaned his chins on his fists. "As to that—ask the Queen's Surgeon, here."

She turned her head. Sir William Harvey's darkly brilliant eyes met hers.

"He is Queen's Surgeon, it's common College gossip."

"Madam, how else can I get protection for my researches? General Olivia will have all bodies religiously buried, I can get no help there."

The Lord-Architect coughed and blew his nose between his fingers. The White Crow gave him a look of utter disgust. He gestured at Harvey:

"Well, rot it! Am I right?"

"The royal family have always been able to touch for the Kings' Evil," Sir William Harvey said. "Because, passed down from generation to generation, they carry that disease themselves. Except that in them it's not fatal; and this ability to carry it harmlessly is what, I think, they pass on with their touch. You understand that the disease has lesions, sores, that allow such contact of vital spirits between her and her petitioners; so that even were there no apparent blood, she would still heal."

He shrugged, finally.

"Of course, none of that royal line live much past forty, and most go soft-witted in the last year or so. If I were a man of science who did *not* value my head, I would tell Carola to adopt an heir. As it is, I praise the blood-royal for its noble healing qualities."

"That's *it*. The newest Entered Apprentice could see it! 'Mystical virtues,' my arse. Where were my wits?" The Lord-Architect reached across and wrapped the White

Crow's hands within his own. She winced at his grip. His booming voice dropped to a low rumble:

"This city has a perfectly respectable tradition of blood-consecration, and for centuries they've been feeding the earth—what? Diseased blood! Of all the whoreson, stupid, rat-arsed, pox-ridden idiocy! No wonder the place is subject to demonic infestation. It's a wonder they can stand one brick on another!"

VIII

"I have probably heard as much as I should, unless this is College business."

His chair scraped brickwork as Sir William Harvey stood. His bow was a bird-quick movement of the head. Still seated, the White Crow reached across and shook his hand: a thin and tenaciously strong grip.

"Thank you, sir."

The Lord-Architect, holding his black brocade frock-coat open and burrowing in an inside front pocket, lifted his head long enough to say, "My regards to young Janou, if you ever hear from any others of this pox-rotten College."

"Sir: of course."

She watched the small man's back as he threaded a way through the crowd that, almost by Brownian motion, began a drift towards the largest vault. White tablecloths and iron tableware shone, beyond the next arch. Smells of cooked pig, quail, roots, and gravy heated the air.

The Lord-Architect took out his hip-flask and lifted it to his lips.

"So you're to go to the Protector . . ." The White Crow hooked up one foot onto the table's edge, clasped her booted ankle, and rested her chin on her knee. "And say: madam,

you stand in need of Carola's blood-royal, because I see no
way to banish these demonic manifestations but by use of
this diseased blood. So you must agree to whatever terms
the Queen may make, when she hears of it?—no:"

Her finger stabbed the air.

"No . . . There'll be enough of her father's by-blows in
the commonwealth that the Queen isn't the only one with
such blood. Do you see Carola summoning up the energy
or the courage to spill her blood on the eye of the sun?
They'll search for some poor bastard of the last reign and
use them."

"No." Casaubon coughed. "Not at all that simple."

"Why not?"

The Lord-Architect Casaubon sneezed and wiped his nose
on the sopping lace-ruffles at his cuff.

"Go home." She prodded his bolster-arm. He coughed
again, resonantly; and she laid her hand across his forehead,
brushing aside sweat-soaked hair. "I'll come back in an hour
and make a Chemicall Decoction. At least I know which of
the planetary *numina* will cure influenza. Casaubon, will you
listen to reason?"

"I don't want to leave you." His breath touched her hand
as she lowered her arm. Hot and moist. He coughed again,
cheeks reddening.

"Will you go home in the carriage now, or shall I wheel
you home in a cart later? I would sooner," she said, changing
from humour to seriousness in the space of a breath, "have
someone else in the house with Jared and the baby, apart
from Kitterage. Will you go?"

"Of c—as*shuuu!*" The Lord-Architect stood up, swayed as
he threw his muffler round his neck, and bent to plant a
snot-wet kiss on the White Crow's hand. "Of course I will,
little one. You may trust me implicitly."

"The trouble is," the White Crow said morosely, wiping
her hand on the back of her breeches, "that I do."

She watched his teetering bulk stagger away. The fat man
ducked his head as he passed under the wine-vault's arches,

knocking with his shoulder a cask that two men and a woman had to grab and replace. A last glimpse of copper-red hair and stained black brocade: she lost him in the crowd.

She turned, walking through into the main vault. Long tables lined the walls. Fires glowed in heavy braziers. It washed over her, the noise of more than forty men and women gathered talking, waiting to be called to table. She nodded acknowledgements; greetings.

"Valentine White Crow."

Hot wire pulled itself tight from throat to gut.

She turned her head. Desire-of-the-Lord Guillaime stood with her gloveless hands outstretched to a brazier. A young woman, not tall; all her thin body bundled up in torn skirts, layers of shirts, a dark greatcoat a size too large. Snow clung to her black hair, melting. "I was searching for you."

"What do you want?"

"Is something the matter?"

The White Crow hugged her arms across her body. The doublet's studs chilled her hands. "Possibly I'm coming down with the influenza. Well?"

The young woman's blue-mottled fingers moved to her coat, unfastening buttons slowly. She gave a slow smile. "I would like something to drink."

The White Crow reached out and took hold of the woman's elbow, the black cloth rough under her hand. Pressure steered Guillaime out of the crowd's main flow, into the space between two wine-casks taller than carriages. She brushed the young woman's frozen fingers away and unfastened the coat herself.

"There."

She reached across, taking a pewter mug, and twisted the wine-cask's top to fill it. Claret glistened. The surface of the dark liquid shook. The White Crow steadied her hand and lifted it, drank a mouthful, and passed it over.

"Now."

"Our friend sends me to make the arrangements for your 'gift.' "

The quiet, distinct voice carried no further than a yard.
Using both hands, the young woman brought the pewter
mug to her mouth and drank. She lifted her head. A red
stain half-mooned the infinitesimally fine hairs above her
upper lip. The White Crow noted the flush beginning to
burn under the fine skin of her cheeks. Little trace of bruises
now.

"I'll want more authority than just your word."

Closed lips moved in a smile; all the warmth of that in
eyes that lowered, flicked up again; challenging.

"You expect the royal Seal?"

The young woman bent and put the mug by her feet, a
motion that carried her intense gaze across the assembled
feasters. She plunged both hands into her greatcoat-pockets,
standing with her weight back on one heel, the other hacking at the flagstones.

"I come with a password. *Newgate.* Will that serve?"

The White Crow pursed her lips and nodded slowly.

"Very well. What arrangements?"

"The coin's ballast in your carriage. Make her a gift of the
carriage and horses. Many courtiers do more to gain favour.
It won't draw suspicion. Nor it won't seem too easy to her."

"Your Protector's a fool. Giving her money. It'll break the
stalemate, there'll be real war—"

"She knows the godless woman better. So do I. I'm privy
to her plans for escape."

"You?"

Melted droplets of snow stood in the young woman's hair,
she standing self-possessed with her hands stretched out to
the brazier's red coals. The hems of her skirts were soaked
knee-high with black slush. She shivered: a glimpse of flesh
between coat-collar and muffler struck by draughts. Her
upper lip curved, lifting.

"She'll give anything to be out of house-arrest at Whitehall. She plans to be across the Narrow Sea and in her
cousin's court before you can say exiled monarch. And stay

there drinking, and going with harlots, and dreaming of the return she'll never make . . ."

Teasing, acid, her tone flicked the White Crow's temper raw.

"Nothing but gossip, I see. But true enough, I don't doubt. Well? That's all. You can go. What else is there?"

The young woman leaned narrow shoulders back against the great cask's curving staves. "You're a Master-Physician."

". . . The examination. Yes. Yes . . . Come to me tomorrow."

Light glinted on brown leather and studs; on the tiny white pin-feathers at the White Crow's fair-skinned temples.

"Before noon. Abiathar will be out reprovisioning, but if you come to the front of the house, I'll let you in."

Black lashes lifted. Eyes that seemed of no colour save brightness caught firelight.

A fiddle squeaked in the night air. William Lilly leaned forward into the cold wind, walking homeward; cloak bundled firmly around him. Snow slid cold and wet across his cheeks.

Ahead, a great bonfire blazed. Snow hissed, floating down from the darkness and falling, consumed, into the flames. Firelight leaped on the paving, on the crowds; sent men's shadows long into the colonnades and porticos of the convent-garden.

"In truth, the skies being so obscured, I had forgot it."

His boot-heels rang on the wet cobbles. He skidded in the slush, walking quickly to keep up with Sir William Harvey and the red-haired woman. The clock up on the portico chimed ten. A weathercock called "All's-well!" He tucked his mittened hands under his tightly bundled cloak.

"This new comet throws out all computations. It hangs in the Sign of the Archer now, about the hour of ten; moves towards the Greene Lyon." Cold air dried his throat. He coughed. "What charts I've drawn you, I can't guarantee."

She turned and faced him, walking backwards for a few paces on the slick, frozen cobbles. The brown cloak swirled to briefly disclose boots, breeches, and the heavy studded brown leather doublet. No sword-belt, no blade. Beyond her, men and women danced and passed bottles; dogs barked. Torch- and firelight shone on her barleyrow Scholars' braids.

"I understand, Master Lilly. I had little hope of astral *magia* answering this, in any case. We need true geomancy."

From the other side of her the small man growled, "Sekhmet's Comet makes all unpredictable. And portends no great good to any."

"As you say, Master Harvey. Now: my way parts with yours here—"

"*Surgeons!*"

Glass smashed.

Lilly stared down at the fan-shaped spray of fragments, each catching the light; sharp edges sinking into slush. High above, the weathervane's cry shifted: "*Beware!*"

He fumbled his coat open, the hilt of his sword cold even through kid-leather bindings. A voice in the crowd around the fire shrieked. "Harvey! It's Butcher Harvey!"

The small man pulled up the collar of his black coat. His powdered hair slipped from its black-ribbon tie. "Whoreson excremental rogues—About: we'll go by Henrietta Street."

The redhaired woman nodded, walking back steadily and quickly beside the astrologer. Head down, her eyes glittered in the bonfire's light. He followed her up steps and under the portico's cover.

"Too late."

A stone ricochetted from a pillar, skittering into the colonnade. A man swore. The crowd jerked: a living thing, all its chirascuro pieces of man, child, woman, and dog eddying suddenly like a flock of rooks.

"Their numbers are too great." Lilly rested his rapier's point on the flagstones. "Madam, if you can—"

Pain stabbed bitter on his tongue.

A hand under his arm dragged him up. Heat hammered his face. His back, snow-wet from falling down, froze, cloth clinging damply to his spine and calves. He grabbed for his dropped rapier. His hands knocked cold cobblestones.

"What . . .?"

Her fingers touched the side of his head and he winced with the pain of the unseen wound. He looked stupidly down at his empty hand.

"Portending ill."

White flakes floated slowly down from the darkness. Fire's orange and red seared against the blue dusk. Logs spat, burning. A rim of blue flame rippled down the planks of a cart, thrown on to make festival fire. A dozen men ran towards him.

"Whoreson bastards!" Harvey yelled, cudgel in one hand, rapier in the other, darting out between the pillars. Swords hit. Metal clanged, loud as any smithy, echoing back from stone. A cart swung up and over, crashing down: a woman launched herself off the top as it fell and struck a tall man between the shoulder-blades. Both fell, lost in the mêlée.

A bottle crashed against the wall beside him.

"A pox!" The redhaired woman picked splinters of glass off her sleeves.

"Madam Roseveare!"

Her face shone, blank with excitement. She moved from foot to foot, hands lightly clenched as if around the hilts of a sword and Florentine dagger. Her eyes fixed on the inexpert cut and parry of the brawl. She grinned and showed all her teeth.

"Oh, I wish—"

The woman abruptly spun round, slid down with her back to a pillar's shelter, and locked one hand in the other's grip. He stood dizzily above her. Shouts blasted his ears. A body knocked against him, jolting him: William Harvey slid to his knees, back in the pillar's shadow. Breathless, he grinned.

"Look out, they come. They mean to beat and kill me, I think."

"Then don't assist them to it!" Lilly grabbed the small man's shoulder. Fear turned over cold in his stomach. "Madam, what can you do?"

She looked up and he met her abstracted gaze: a little humourous, a little sad.

"I can wish I carried a sword, Master Lilly."

Exasperated, he said, "But you do not. Madam—"

"It isn't the ability to defend myself, or others, that I miss. Although there are times when a pistol or sword would be of more immediate service than *magia*. Yes."

She smiled painfully.

"I miss fighting."

Her eyes bright, she leaned forward, rocking just slightly, movements of muscles restrained. Unseen, someone shouted. A hard object hit the wall. A sudden rush of foot-steps halted. Each noise made her eyes flick sideways, seeking.

A musket crashed, shot exploding across the dark sky in warning. Noise sang in his ears.

"Now that's enough." The woman stood.

Sir William Harvey grunted and got to his feet. "My apologies for this."

The woman touched him lightly on the shoulder. She turned to face the convent-garden square. Snow fell on the rioting crowd, the speed and solidity of the flakes ignored.

She reached up and drew a long pin from her hair. Gold sparkled. Without hesitation she held up her left hand, and thrust the pin through the centre of her palm. She dropped to one knee. Her bloodied fingers traced sigils in the frozen slush and on hard-trodden ice.

Silence.

The night darkened. Icy air breathed in his face. Lilly rubbed his eyes. "Madam, well done!"

Thickening snow fell faster. A sharp crack echoed. He stepped back, thinking it a stone; another fell, and another.

Hailstones plummeted down.

The night skies opened. Within three heartbeats he could

hear nothing but a million hailstones hiss and crack, splintering down on cobblestones; sky thickly grey over the convent-garden walls; the bonfires guttering to extinction. Splinters of ice shrapnelled the pillars.

In the open square men and women covered their heads with their hands, running abjectly for shelter.

Hailstones drummed. The woman hissed between her teeth, tugging the needle from her hand. The skin of her palm pulled up as the metal withdrew. Blood welled. She sat down hard in the slush, on the stone under the portico, legs sprawling; her face running with sweat.

Her voice, when it came, rasped with utter exhaustion:

"I was ten years a trained Scholar-Soldier. I was the best they had with a blade. Now I'm Master-Physician and no soldier . . . Don't think I never knew who I injured, or what it meant, or how much I risked. *I miss fighting.* I miss all the dangers of a duel. It was—it's like air and sunlight to me."

A new morning chilled her. Olivia touched a gauntlet to the blood-marked stone and straightened. Soldiers crowded the construction-site behind her, pikes and crossbows ready under a cold and brilliant sky.

The workman's body lay already shrouded.

"And no answer from Master Casaubon?"

Humility Talbot shook his head.

"I'll have an answer today," she said grimly, "if I have to go for it myself."

The Lord-Architect lifted one large, bare foot from the bowl of hot water, examined it morosely through the steam, and sneezed. His foot thumped down. Water flew across floorboards and bedroom rug.

"I am *perfectly* well!"

The woman sat back on her heels. She brushed at her now-wet shirt with a bandaged left hand. "Of course you are. Or at least, you will be."

Aromatic herbs floated in the steaming bowl. He sniffed. Under his vast nightdress, talismans on chains hung hot against his skin. As he watched, she unwrapped the rough bandage and squeezed a drop of blood from her palm into the water.

"Will that cure me?" he croaked hopefully.

"That and staying in bed for the next twenty-four hours."

"I have no intention of going back to bed!" Casaubon paused; took out his handkerchief; blew a long, wet, trumpet-blast; and surveyed the result dismally.

"Except," he finished weakly, "possibly for the next twenty-four hours."

The Queen and Sir Denzil Waldegrave stood at one window of the Whitehall Palace, looking down into the snow-choked yard. Carola cradled a bottle of Madeira. A team of four horses strained at the crack of a whip. The driver, a lanky fair-haired countryman, pulled the team up on treacherous ice. Washed, if not polished, the elderly coach shone in the morning light.

"Odds me, madam, a rare present."

"More than you know." The swarthy woman laughed, clinking bottle to windowpane, and pushing the window open. Freezing air cleared the fug of the night's marathon card-game. Waldegrave shuddered, pale.

"We will have you stow Roseveare's gift safely away. Very safely." Carola hesitated. She pointed with one blue-silk-clad arm. "Sir, who's that? With yonder little puritan girl."

Below in the yard, the woman Guillaime entered under the arch and stopped dead. A gentleman-mercenary, one among many entering the Palace for the morning's audience, took off his tricorne hat and bowed. Brown curls glinted. The young woman straight-armed past him, skidding in the snow. His guffaw floated up to Carola.

"Captain Calmady, ma'am. A mercenary. An incurable violent man." Denzil Waldegrave inclined his head as the man saluted the Queen. "He raped the girl and must hang for it, since the woman Olivia has him under her arrest."

She lifted the bottle to her lips and drank the dregs. A faint cheer drifted up from the crowd in the courtyard. She waved carelessly, turning from the window.

"The 'Protector' is holding trial on one of our subjects?"

"A mercenary, your Majesty. And, the situation being how it is, it would hardly be politic to complain."

She turned on him a face from which all humour and all laziness vanished.

"The Queen's writ still runs in this commonwealth, does it not? The Queen's justice is the fount of all justice?"

"Yes, madam, but—"

"Arrest Captain Calmady. Find witnesses and have him brought to trial. It may prove politic," the swarthy woman considered, "to have what Justice the woman Olivia approves of on the bench, but we will have no man tried but by the laws of this commonwealth, and they, after all revolts and confusions, remain *mine*."

Desire walked to stand by the window.

The White Crow hesitated, closing the door. Noon's snow-reflected brightness shone in on the young woman's face, but called out no fire from the matt darkness of her hair. Each hand clasped an elbow. Her chin was sunk into the collar of her coat.

The door closed with a creak.

"I said I'd examine you, didn't I? Yes . . ."

The White Crow shivered, crossing to the fire and squatting down to place fresh coals. The scent of seacoal permeated the air. Frost-patterns starred the window-glass.

"I would know, if I carry a child? Or a disease?"

A quiet voice, low and resonant. The White Crow straightened. In some interest, she looked down at her fingers. They shook. She rubbed her hands together, a slight smile on her face; taking a brief glance around the room.

Books piled on window-seat, oaken chair, and floor. Bundles of herbs lay scattered across the big desk, together with half-incised talismans. She absently cleared the remnants of an amulet to one side, and tapped her finger to her lips, gaze moving along the meagre row of bottles on the shelf above the workbench.

"Sit down. The couch, there. Have you eaten today?"

"Nothing."

"Good."

Three bottle-necks between her fingers, the White Crow pulled the cork from a fourth with her teeth as she walked across the room. She held out the blue-white glass container.

"Do I drink it?" The young woman held the bottle, sinking to sit on the couch. White linen creased where she sat. The White Crow took the cork from between her teeth.

"Drink from one, spit in t'other. Then we'll wait. Trust me."

"I already trusted you once." Mocking, calculating: Desire's eyes shone. "At Roseveare. You failed me."

"You can't trade on that forever."

"Can I not?"

"Oh, but *you* . . ." A wealth of tones in that word: speculation, resentment, admiration, envy. The White Crow rested her knee up on the couch, the bottles in her left hand clinking softly. Recalled, she held each up to the window-light in turn; shook each; and placed them one at a time on the floor.

"I'll have to examine you."

The young woman lowered the bottle, frowning a little. A tongue-tip flicked out, clearing the last oily liquid from her lips. Noon leached colour from her pale, prominent cheekbones; shadowed her eyes with sepia and her lips with blue.

The White Crow leaned weight on her knee that rested on the couch. Close enough to breathe in all the scents of her—herb-comfrey, and the rankness of just-stale sweat—she watched Desire's fingers unknot the clasp of her coat.

Desire pulled her arms from the sleeves, awkward as a child.

A black, ragged doublet came next; buttoned at every second or third button. A grey shirt, clean but faded. Desire pulled her shoulders up, down; sliding the cloth free. Her hands dropped to her belt. She tugged loose the sash of a ragged, full skirt.

The White Crow slipped. Her knee skidded from the couch's linen cover. One hand, flying out for balance, knocked against the young woman's arm.

The air of the room tingled: hot with fire, cold with snow. Frozen condensation whorled the windowpane. A coal snapped in the grate. Her face burned. With hands now perfectly steady she reached out and unbuttoned the young woman's thin cotton shirt.

Black eyes glinted. One of the corners of her pale lips tugged up: as it might be Desire smiled.

The White Crow cupped her hands over the young woman's shoulders, every crease of the last white, sleeveless shirt pressing her palms. She slid her hands down around the small, heavy breasts; traced the sharpness of ribs; held her with one hand to each hip. Each impossible touch broke barriers between possibility and actuality.

Shaking, heightened; simultaneously aware and with a complete sense of unreality, she pulled the girl to her feet and tore at the buttons fastening her cobweb-thin shirt.

The young woman stood stiff, resistant.

"*Trust* me!" The White Crow reached out, knotting fists in the unbound masses of Desire's coarse black hair, pulling her head forward and kissing her fiercely.

One heel skidded on the floor: a bottle shattered.

The White Crow grabbed and fumbled her grip; ripped the sleeveless shirt, and lowered her mouth to lick at the sweat on the curve of Desire's shoulder. Smooth here, rough there with old scar-tissue: tasting of all sweetness, all sour discordancies of taste.

Breath hissed in her throat.

She sat back up onto one heel, staring the young woman in the face. Skin tingled. Silence sang, waiting for the shout that would break it.

The fire, the linen couch, the deserted floor of the house: all determined, all planned. To end here, with a face heavy-lidded, black and delicate lashes lowered. Feeding on itself now, the desire reified by its first act.

Deliberately moving the remaining bottles aside, she pushed the young woman's body back on the couch. Her hands dug to feel the heat of flesh across the slender back. She pushed her unbandaged hand under the waistband of the young woman's black skirt, sliding fingers across the soft flesh of her belly, fighting the resistance of cloth, fingers prodding between her thighs.

"I'm not—!"

An elbow hit her jaw and ear. Jarred, she shook her head to clear it.

"—not healed yet; it *hurts*—"

The White Crow recovered her free hand from under the solidity of flesh. She pulled at her own shirt, buttons flying. Some fierce grin fired her. She pulled the young woman's head to her breast, feeling the shiver of warm breath across her nipple; reached down and tugged her belt-buckle undone with a bandaged hand. Desire struggled.

"—*hurts!*"

A shrill whisper.

"I'll be careful. Trust me. Trust me."

The White Crow forced her down, one arm now across Desire's collarbone, pinning her. A knee hit her shoulder. Her breeches slid down her hips, bare flesh shivering in the winter room.

"You're beautiful!"

Pressed bare breast to belly, sweat-slick, hand thrusting still between the young woman's legs, rubbing soft and damp hair; fingers probing hot, slick interior flesh. The White Crow caught her breath, dipped her head and bit roughly at warm flesh: at white-scarred arms and prominent ribs; mouthing saliva across small, heavy breasts.

The Protector-General Olivia lifted her gloved hand to knock on the door of Roseveare House. It swung open. She nodded briefly to the two black-mantled soldiers. They took up unobtrusive posts along the Court, cursing the deep snow. She stepped over the threshold.

Somewhere distantly upstairs, a bottle smashed.

She swung the door to and walked swiftly through the hall. One hand rested at the belt of her buff coat, on a pistol's butt. Stairs went up into gloom. She climbed, alert for further sound.

Silence.

Closed doors confronted her on the first floor. About to push one open at random, hand on the latch, she heard a creak from the bannisters of the landing above.

The Lord-Architect Casaubon leaned over, draped in the folds of a scarlet-and-gold nightgown, and with a tasselled nightcap on his head.

"No servants, master architect?"

The fat man wiped his eyes, fingering yellow sleep-grit from the corners. He stuck his finger in his mouth, sucked and removed it. "Servants' day off, rot 'em. Valentine should answer the *magia*-wards. I don't know what she can be thinking of. I, myself, am far too ill to leave my bed—"

"I need to know about the eye of the sun, Master Casaubon. Now. When I returned to the Tower this morning, I found your written report."

"You'd better come up."

He swirled yards of cloth about his arms, bundling himself up and raising the hem of the gown of his stockinged calves. Olivia chuckled. She took the stairs two at a time, following him into a bright room.

"However, I *was* working." The Lord-Architect pried up

the blankets on the immense four-poster bed and climbed back in.

Blueprints tipped across the blankets. Plans covered the bed, the floor; hung pinned to the bed's draperies, and crackled under the Lord-Architect as he leaned back against the pillows. He wiped his red nose.

Olivia cleared a space and seated herself on the foot of the bed. "I want answers if you have them, educated guesses if you don't."

"Guesses?" He unrolled a six-foot plan across his lap, pinning down the end with a jar of wintergreen ointment. "I can guarantee you, the burglaries and thefts of St. Sophia will drop by two-thirds when you allow me to make alteration to the Rookery tenements." His fat finger prodded the paper. "With these building alterations I can guarantee a lessening in the crimes committed there."

"The poor of this town don't need lessoning in crime."

"Wittily said."

Olivia stripped off her gloves. She pushed the wispy yellow-white hair away from her face. "The Rookeries are corrupt. Master Casaubon, men are made of sin. I don't think you'll deny them the desire to thieve by denying them one walkway to reach a window by, or one more exit by which to flee. Now: the temple—"

"Pox rot you, they're not different! Structures compel—"

The man broke into a fit of coughing. The Protector steadied herself on the bed, her feet not quite touching the floor. Heaped blankets shook, covering the immense legs, stomach, and torso of the man in the bed; he peering down at her red-faced, watery-eyed.

"Master Casaubon, the eye of the sun is builded according to those proportions and rules that govern the universe; it has within it an outer light to mirror man's Inner Light; it is a *temple,* and not a slum!"

She stood up, pacing the room.

"Your report says that I need the blood-royal and that I can't use it because it is diseased. *Why* can it not be used?

What else is there? Are the Rookeries your price for telling me?"

"The Rookeries slums are something you'll have me do if you want to save your tenants from what *you'd* call opportunities to sin. Death and furies!" He sat up in bed, a volcano-lava of sheets and blankets spilling down. A smell of sweat and ointment breathed across her.

"Master Casaubon: the eye of the sun!"

"This city's had its temples consecrated by the royal-bloodline for how long? Centuries?" He nodded massive satisfaction. "The foundations of the earth have reached saturation point. Hereditary—that blood carries a virus. By now it attracts as much demonic power as it dispels."

"Carola's blood feeds demons." She tapped her gloves against her bulbous chin. "Consecrates ground—and attracts demons. And yet the ground must be consecrated. I don't see the answer."

"Blindingly simple." The large man spread his hands. "Build it in another city."

"What?"

"Your Carola." He sniffed. "The Sun Monarch herself couldn't build a temple to the sun in this city! No matter how harmonic the proportions, how much in conformity with the Universal Architect's laws, you'll have an infestation of demons before the pox-rotted foundations are sunk. They've been taught to expect it."

She stopped with one hand holding the bottom poster of the bed.

"I must build here. I must build in the capital."

"Dammit, you can't!"

"Our Lord's light, and the light of reason, have to be manifest *here*." Her hand closed hard on the carved wood. The edges bit into her fingers. "We're the only legitimate protection against the godless woman's tyranny, master architect; and we can only prove ourselves legitimate in this ancient seat of government. I must be able to complete the building."

"You may. Eventually. And have to call in a demolition expert inside a decade to get rid of the thing."

"That dangerous?"

"I've seen corruptive architecture before." The fat man leaned back against stacked pillows. The room's light altered, chilling to sepia; and she glanced at the window and saw, tiny and slow, black specks spiralling down against a yellow sky. Fire snapped in the grate. Somewhere in the depths of Roseveare House, a door slammed.

"You have a plain choice." The Lord-Architect grunted, swinging his legs down and feeling with his feet for red-heeled slippers. "Use some poor royal bastard's blood, build the place, and have it corrupt more of its worshippers than it heals. Or don't use it, and have the building collapse. Or, by the Great Architect's anus, build it in some other city!"

Olivia made a wry mouth.

"That's no choice at all. Obviously I cannot choose any of these actions—and yet—I must choose."

The Lord-Architect plodded back up the stairs from seeing Olivia out. He paused at the door to the herb-room.

"Little one?"

The White Crow, visible thorugh the now-open door, sat up on the couch. The rucked-up sheet tangled her ankles. One elbow rested on her knee, and her forehead on her fist. Her shirt hung open, two buttonholes torn, and her unbuckled breeches slid down over her hips; brown cloth against fair, faintly-freckled skin. She looked up.

"Yes! All right? The answer is yes."

The woman stood. The covering sheet slid from the couch to the dusty floorboards. She made to step over, holding up her breeches; half-halted, and bent to pick up a bottle. She held it up to the light as she walked across to the bench, shook it, eyes narrowing.

"Veneral infection. Nothing too serious; I can make her an infusion to clear it up. I must let her know. *Casaubon—*"

She slammed the bottle down, turned.

The Lord-Architect walked across the creaking floorboards to her, and cupped her chin in large, strong fingers. His ink-stained thumb rubbed her jaw thoughtfully.

"Did you?"

She pulled away. *"Yes!"*

The Lord-Architect eased himself down into the large chair beside the hearth, sinking into voluminous night-robes. His gaze never shifted from her face. She, finished with buttoning herself and now buckling her belt, sat in the window-seat.

"I don't love her."

The White Crow rested her chin on her wrists, staring down from the window-ledge as she talked. On the other side of chill glass, snow fell into Roseveare Court, and torches flared gold on the shoe-tracks and bookstalls and open bookshop doorways. Two black-mantled soldiers and a woman in a buff coat trampled the snow towards the main thoroughfare.

"I *hurt* her. She obsesses me. I can't tell you that she won't always do that."

Casaubon sat still. His eyes narrowed very slightly.

"I can't give her up," the White Crow added, "and I'll die if I don't have you. I don't even pretend that that's fair."

A tiny snap sounded in the room, in the silence that snow produces, muffling all other sound. The Lord-Architect looked down at the louse nipped between his thumb-nails, and smeared the body on his furred nightgown. Thighs spread, arms resting back on the arms of the chair that his body barely fitted, he looked up at the White Crow over a mountain of belly.

"I didn't win you for my beauty." Pink coloured his creased cheeks. He looked at her sadly. "I made you laugh. I make myself indispensable, because I can always make the melancholy Valentine laugh. But, of course, beginning so, you always see me so. I make you merry. There's an end to it."

The White Crow lifted her head from her arms, and looked at him over her shoulder. "You underestimate me. I know what you are. You're the man who pretends to be my solid rock and foundation, and proves ultimately as flighty and eccentric as—as anyone could wish. Did it never occur to you that I love you *because* you're an infuriating lunatic?"

The Lord-Architect cocked one dark-red eyebrow in her direction, paused for a calculated moment, and remarked, "No. But I had hopes."

"That's *exactly*—*that's* what I—you're the only man I know," she said, "who's smarter than I am, and that's something I won't tell you every day. But she . . ."

Casaubon rumbled. "Did you really think I would be complaisant enough, or sufficiently insecure, to say that I would share you?"

"You may have to. For the moment, anyway."

The Lord-Architect leaned back, to the creak of oakwood, and gave her his most childlike and innocent gaze. "You may think so."

She shifted to her feet in one easy movement, tugging her belt straight as she walked to the door and lifted her cloak from the door-hook. She swung the cloak, muffling herself to the ears, and then stopped with her hand on the jamb as she went out.

"Thank you," she said, "for not mentioning Jared and the baby."

IX

T owards the middle of that same afternoon, with the snow easing and people once more on the streets, the Lady Arbella Lacey swaggered out of the little streets behind Eleanor's Cross. A keen wind cut at her nose, cheeks, and chin.

"Sir!" She caught the elbow of a man in frock-coat and plumed hat. "Is there a hostelry hereabouts where an honest soldier can get a drink? And would you have a copper for a woman who's fought hard in the late wars?"

She let her shabby velvet cloak slip back and show the sword in its hanger at her side. Cold reddened her bare fingers. She sniffed and wiped her nose, mucus running from the keen air and from half a day's drinking.

"There. That's all." The elderly man, somewhere between sullenness and good humour, pressed cold coins into her hand. "My child went for a soldier, too; I'd not willingly see her comrades beg. And to your question—no, there is no inn hereabouts for honest soldiers, but there is *The New-Founde Land Arms* down yonder that will take a mercenary's coin."

"The Bull bless you, sir!" Arbella Lacy grinned, breath huffing onto the cold air. "Mercenaries, say you? Yonder there? I recognise the nags outside; you've found me my comrades and I bless you for it—"

"No more money. Go."

The man shuffled away. He leaned heavily on his ebony cane. Trooper Arbella Lacey amused herself for several steps with a parody of his walk, slipped, swore to herself, and plodded through the broken snow down towards the Whitehall Palace and the inn.

She stopped in the hostelry's porch to kick clogged snow from her boots. Some noise in the almost impassable road behind her made her turn, and narrow her streaming eyes as she stared back across Whitehall.

She spun to kick the inn's door open and rush inside.

A quarter of a mile away in the kitchens of Roseveare House, the White Crow cradled her sweat-damp baby in the crook of her arm. Exhausted, it whimpered; the whimper sawing up the scale towards a full-scale scream.

"Oh, shit." She hefted the baby gently in both arms, glancing at Abiathar with red-rimmed eyes. "You wouldn't think it had the energy, would you? Three solid hours . . . I'll see if I can feed her."

"You'll feed her anger with your milk."

"If I wanted blame I'd have stayed upstairs." The White Crow unlaced her doublet without looking at the older woman, pulled the ties on her shirt, and offered the baby her nipple. The child refused, square-mouthed, beating with clenched fists.

"Here." Abiathar reached down and lifted the child. Jadis fumbled uselessly at the woman's bodice for some moments, murmured indignation, and slid off into a half-doze. "She knows your anger. It's in your touch."

The White Crow ignored her own resentment and looked up at Abiathar. The older woman walked back and forth in front of the kitchen range, humming. Fire's shadows and winter afternoon light dappled the baby's bright hair.

"Did my husband say where he was going when he left?"

Abiathar shook her head. "No word. I ast him if he wanted Kitterage and a hired coach, but he said no. Will he have gone to his old building site, then?"

She paused, looking down into the baby's face, and added, "Won't be the first Roseveare to have married an odd man, you won't."

"I'll leave her and Jared with you."

Her face burned warmer than the kitchen stove could account for, feeling the country woman's gaze on her.

"For an hour or so. I'll walk over to the site and find him. I want . . ." She stood and stretched out her arms, feeling bones click and tendons stretch. "I've done what *I* came to London to do. *He's* been to that site twice, and I don't know if he's any closer to an answer than when we came. I want to know how much longer we have to stay."

Half a mile south of Roseveare, Shrine Paddifer leaned his elbows on the table in the St. Sophia communal dining-room.

"The St. Sophia commune has petitioned the Protector for aid against criminals." He brushed his short grey hair out of his eyes. "As we petitioned for the Queen's grace in the same matter, not so long since. All the blocks suffer the depredations of priggers, Abraham-men, footpads, and Tall Men. We tried our own vigilante patrols, to little effect."

The very large man seated opposite coughed resonantly. "The whole pox-rotten place invites 'em in! Provides walk-ways, blind corners, unlit passages; corridors where no one can see attacks; a dozen paths to flee by. The old proverb has it: *postern doors make thieves and whores.*"

The Lord-Architect Casaubon occupied all one side of the oak-panelled bench opposite, a broken meat-pie steaming on a dish before him. He waved an emphatic hand, meat and pastry held between large fingers.

"Madam Olivia will shortly be in need of—" Meat slipped, the Lord-Architect made a swift bite at it; grease rolled down his chin. "—much in need of a worthy building proj-

ect. A public one. Rot it, if she cleans up St. Sophia, she'll
look sweet in the City's eyes! That's to your good, Master
Paddifer. Take advantage of it."

He sniffed, beaming, and wiped his nose on the back of
one lace-ruffled cuff.

"You must excuse me. Haven't been well. No appetite."

Shrine Paddifer eased as far back against the oak partition
as possible, wiping at his spattered black shirt and under-
shirts. Raw wood, graffiti-hacked, caught threads in his
clothing. Voices rang out loudly from the room's other tables, in their own cubicles; and a pair of children in layers
of rags ran from the battered kitchen door to the far wall,
sliding on slush-wet flagstones.

"You spoke of something attendant on this. A bargain?"

"A private bargain."

The man scratched at his straggling cropped hair,
smearing gravy and a fragment of mushroom in the copper-
red strands. His lace collar untied, and buttons undone on
his viridian waistcoat, the Lord-Architect leaned back with
a contented sigh. Shrine Paddifer reached across and poured
another cup of acorn-coffee.

"There was born and bred in St. Sophia a young woman
by the name of Guillaime."

The faintest lift of tone implied a question. Shrine Paddifer, surprised, nodded. "Yes. Down in the third tenement-
block."

The big man's hand slammed down on the table. "Damnation, I knew it! Master Paddifer, I recognised her as a Rook-
ery-bird by her dress."

A smile spread across his face, creasing the rolls of fat
around his blue eyes: immensely and innocently pleased
with himself. Shrine Paddifer abandoned any idea of being
insulted. He allowed himself an ironical smile.

"We give the Protector a number of her best people.
What about Desire-of-the-Lord Guillaime, master architect?
How is she part of the bargain for your services?"

Foosteps clumped across the floor above. A child cried.

Two young men and a woman clattered down the narrow, winding stairs; threw the outer door open to afternoon's pale light as they ran into the yard. Shrine Paddifer eased himself out from behind the table and walked to close the door.

Behind him, the deep voice rumbled:

"I shall need to consult with the Sun of Science on the blueprints—that is, the Head of the Byzantine College. Young Mistress Guillaime seems very trustworthy. I want her to act as my messenger to Byzantium, while I remain here."

The large man buried his nose in the cup of acorn-coffee. Shrine Paddifer returned to the table. Standing, his eyes were much on a level with the seated man's.

"She'll be honoured."

"London can spare her for a few months. Travel broadens experience." The Lord-Architect, as much as possible for a man of his size, hunched down in his green frieze coat. His eyes flicked up and remained on Shrine Paddifer's face: a steady and uncompromising gaze. "That is my condition of employment."

The afternoon light shone winter-brilliant. Desire-of-the-Lord Guillaime lay on her back.

"Put your feet in the stirrups. Now part your knees."

The leather couch chilled her back and buttocks. She shifted awkwardly down. Her bare feet slid into wooden stirrups. Her threadbare shift only covered her breasts and belly, and she put one arm across her face, staring into the welcome dark of flesh.

"Be still."

The immediate chill of grease made her startle. The muscles of her thighs tightened. Cold metal probed between her legs, pushing the walls of her vagina apart. She closed her hands into fists, never wincing. The speculum pushed deep inside, hurting. It halted, moved painfully to one side; moved again and drove deeper.

"Still!"

The Protectorate doctor's instrument snicked vaginal flesh as it withdrew.

"Dress. Wait outside."

She shifted her cramped legs down. She fumbled on layers of skirts, belts, and buckles done up anyhow. An antiseptic scent choked her nostrils. The surgery door creaked as she pushed past it, and in the empty room beyond cupped both hands to her pubis and leaned her head against the cold window-glass. She made one sound, a sob or sharp intake of breath.

Under her hands, cloth warmed, slightly numbing the pain of flesh.

Silence muffled the St. Sophia Rookery. White light blazed from beyond the window. Roofs, gables, all ice-fanged; all familiar. Known streets, trodden into slush and frozen again. Piled drifts of snow against tenement walls all burning with interior diamonds. A faint mist hazed Monmouth Street and the spire clock at the seven road's junction.

Desire-of-the-Lord Guillaime straightened. She brushed wet hair back from her forehead, and adjusted her belt-buckle, and pulled on fingerless leather gloves. She stared down at her discarded coat.

The surgery door opened.

"Master Hargrave?"

The priest-surgeon lifted his head, looking down at her; a tall man, white-haired, and with deep creases in his face. All his old warmth vanished, all consolation gone.

"I *am* ill? She would not tell me, she—"

"Ill? Yes, grievous sick!"

He made to turn, to go back into the surgery. She stepped forward. He caught the side of his white robe, jerking the hem away from her.

"Master Hargrave!"

"The Lord has visited justice on you. Your woman's parts, those parts that tempted the man of blood, are diseased. It is written that *a harlot shall rot in her pride.* Yes, you are sick."

His nostrils widened slightly, whitening.

"You may not go to the Lord for many years. All that time you shall remain in sickness and sores. If the devil give you children, as it may be the man of blood has left his seed in your body, then the children of your body shall carry the disease. You shall become a stink and an abomination. And die, in the end, mad with your sin, the judgement come upon you."

A snowball jarred the window. She tangled her fingers in her hair. Outside, a child shrieked, a dozen more ran, scuffing up snow. They would be making a slide in the old places, outside this surgery and at the Shaftesbury Avenue junction. A horse neighed: a carter swore. Apt enough to make her mouth tremble, a hymn sounded from the nearest of the Rookery's thirty-seven chapels.

"Is there *no* cure?"

He stared down at her: a young woman now, black hair disordered; a shirt buttoned crudely across her small breasts, and belted skirts hanging down to her heeled ankle boots. Her hands in fingerless gloves made fists.

"Cure?"

He bent, scooped up her coat, and threw it into her face. She stepped back, heels clattering.

"Cure! Why speak of cures. Your soul is irredeemably diseased. Desire-of-the-Lord, I knew your mother. The Lord rest her, she doesn't live to see this. I know your father and your grandmother, honest people, who live in the fear of the Lord: think, how will you shame them! No man can cure you of this sin."

She leaned her back against the front door of the surgery.

Staring up into the sun, with no memory of leaving the place.

Away down the road, near one of the brick tenement entrances, a bundled-up girl of perhaps seven drilled a dozen like her: broomsticks for pikes, shovels for muskets; the smallest girl throwing snowballs; four eminently self-righteous boys singing a Protectorate marching hymn.

Her lips moved with ancient memory, mirroring the words.

"Remember the crow is a carrion bird . . ."

Valentine of Roseveare, called White Crow, stopped at the unlocatable murmur. She held her link-torch higher against the early winter dusk.

The site of the eye of the sun spread out around her, deserted.

"Who's there?" With the hand that did not hold the torch, she rubbed finger and thumb together. A rose-light glowed, gleamed with marsh-fire blues and greens. She lowered the flaming brand. The sweat on her right hand crackled, turned to ice.

". . . crow is . . . carrion bird . . ."

The sky shone a dirty, darkening grey. A mist blurred the lines of cranes and gantries, scaffolding platforms and sighting-towers. No man nor woman moved on the site. She trudged forward to where the churned clay-and-slush gave way to sandstone pavement.

Mirror gleamed.

The White Crow held up her hand that flamed blue. The chill of the fire hurt. She stuck the link-torch into a gap between stacked masonry blocks and walked forward without it, her shadow jolting across the inlaid steel and silver of the dome-floor.

The knowledge that work such as could be done in this weather would have finished some two hours gone, and the lack of the Lord-Architect's presence; this and the grey evening might have accounted for the chill on her spirit. The White Crow showed teeth in a fierce smile.

"I know your kind," she said softly, "better than you know me. Show yourself."

Feathers scratched at the underside of glass.

She walked forward on the pavement until she stood where the inset mirrors merged. In the dome to come, this would be the edge of prayer. And from the high opening, sunlight would stream down, illuminating the whole vast interior with a Light of eyes and feathers and angels' wings.

She squatted down on her haunches.

". . . *a carrion bird* . . ."

Practised, she reached a pin from her hair and let blood from her left index finger. Two signs she traced on the sandstone paving. The third, a swift curve with complicated lettering, she wrote on the mirror surface itself.

Mist and ice ran away from the mirror as frost melts at noon.

The White Crow looked down into the clarity beneath.

"The crow is the bird that travels between the living and the dead," she formally stated. "If you have something to show: show. If you have something to tell: tell. But I hear with the ears of *magia*. Lies and trickery will not bite on me."

Black feathers flicked at the underside of the mirror's thick glass. She wasted no time looking up into the London sky for them. A flight of black birds, beaks and talons glinting obsidian-bright; filling all the well of the mirror; and as the flock diminished—

She hovers above a field of bright grass. The white mists of artillery fire blot out horses as they gallop forward; she cannot hear the sound of the guns, but she can hear the caws of crows as the scavengers rob the bodies in the night after when—as always happens after day-long cannonfire— it rains. Rains on the cold, bloody dead.

She recognises uniforms: Protectorate and Royalist.

A coach on a deserted moor is halted, robbed; passengers bludgeoned and left for dead; she is too far from the vision to see, quite, who these people are.

Back alleys, sick beds, camps, sea wrecks; each tantalisingly closer. Almost close enough to see every face, every death.

"You are lying badly . . ."

Her voice is not as steady as she would wish. The White Crow sits for a while on her haunches while the link-torch burns down, watching faces. Because it *may* be a foreshadowing, it may be the warning that proves such fates avoidable, she watches faces, faces by the hundred, men and women in clothing familiar and unfamiliar; and in all those faces, watch as closely as she might, she sees no face at all that she knows.

A plume of white fire hung, still against night's blackness, drowning stars. Bevil Calmady swayed in the cleared middle of the square and stared up at the comet.

Motionless, frozen light.

As if speaking the words could ease him, he recited: " 'A sacrifice to Law's Majesty and an example to all malevolent men—' "

He staggered ankle-deep in new snow, sliding on the packed ice beneath; grabbed at his sword-hilt, and looked dizzily for Gadsbury, Lacey, Rule, Linebaugh: all gone into the comet-lit night.

"Boy!"

An oxyacetylene brightness illuminated the square and the frozen fountains. Ice ridged and rippled. Torches flared. Two linkmen preceded a sedan-chair down the treacherous road. One hauled out a cudgel, torch wavering in his free hand.

A head poked through the sedan-chair window.

"He's no footpad. Set down, set down!"

The carriers—four men, not two—set the chair down in the snow. Ice crunched as the Lord-Architect Casaubon pushed the door open and stepped out.

"What's the matter, boy? Answer. Is it the house?"

Bevil Calmady shook his head, conscious of reporting concisely. "Not Roseveare."

The wind cut under his plumed hat, bobbing one broken ostrich feather. An active, wet cold seared his chin, jaw, and ears. Under the comet's light the large man's hair shone black as shed blood. Bevil Calmady scented elder-flower wine and warm breath.

Apologetic, devastated, he said, "I know there's nothing to be done, sir. It's the Queen's justice. *Can* you help him? He claims you for his friend."

"Damnation, slowly, boy. Slowly. Hold and then tell me."

Sword-buckles and spurs chimed, clotted with ice. Bevil rubbed his gloved hand across his forehead, the kidskin cold and wet.

"His trial. My *father*. They held it this afternoon."

"What, the Protector-General—"

"No, sir. The Queen's men took him."

"The Qu . . ." The fat man squinted under the comet's brilliance, spun a coin to the lead carrier, and hooked his arm around Bevil's shoulder, steering him irresistibly along. "Come to Roseveare. Tell me as you walk. What, rot it, they can't hold any trial, the man's on bail to my house!"

Shudders took Bevil's flesh, deep down inside his belly. The wind sheered through his wool cloak and silk doublet. He moved his shoulders out of the big man's grip.

"I knew nothing of it. Arbella and the company found me, about four of the clock, said, *"We've seen him taken under guard: quick!"* I followed. When we got to the Bailey, it was the Queen's Justice, John Whorewood, a notorious puritan."

"Ah." The Lord-Architect nodded.

"He had bunches of herbs on the bench, to ward off prison-stink!"

Tall gables in St. Martin's Lane blocked the night sky. The comet's light glinted from glass and horn windows. The Lord-Architect's powerful legs thrust through snow, untramelled. His breath smoked on the air. "Tried by a puritan judge, but in the Queen's court. Without witnesses?"

"Oh, yes." Self-assured cynicism slipped. Bevil Calmady clenched his hands. "They'd written depositions as if from the Guillaime bitch. Sir, have you ever heard a man . . . *The sentence is that thou shalt return from hence to New-*

gate prison, and from thence to the place of execution at
Tyburn, where thou shalt hang by the neck till the body be
dead and in the Devil his hands, and the Lord his mercy
on your soul.' "

Bevil stepped aside to avoid the corner of a standing cart,
piled high with grit and shovels for the morning. Someone
coughed at a high window. A feather of applause drifted
from distant theatres.

"My father trained me to remember words." Unacknowl-
edged pain ripped in his stomach. "He told us the bitch-
General would never dare sentence him. Why should her
Majesty want him hanged? I don't understand."

He looked up at the older man, his back stiffening. "Gadsbury says, *Queen's justice.* They drink to the Queen and her
Hangman. Oh, would to God there was anything I could
do!"

"How long has he?"

"Five days. Wednesday next."

Late in empty streets, Bevil pushed heel and toe into ice
to stay upright, his voice as slurred as a drunken man's.
Feeling the knot finally cut that tied Gadsbury, Lacey,
Winslow, himself: the dissolution of the company, gone with
its captain. Or if re-tied, nothing the same.

And Pollexfen Calmady to die.

"What can I do, sir?"

The Lord-Architect Casaubon dug his chins down into his
coat-collar, turning into Roseveare Court and the keen wind.
"Eat before you fall down. I'll take you to the kitchen."

Bevil Calmady blinked water from his eyes. "My father . . ."

"We'll—*Valentine?*"

Stunned with memories, a half-second passed before Bevil
focussed.

The woman sat on a step at the corner of the narrow
street. Her cloak matted dark with melted snow. Red hair,
damp-darkened, dripped ice-water onto fingers without sen-

sation: she rested her face in her hands. Bare flesh, mottled by cold, shuddered.

The big man took three swift strides to reach her. His hands closed around her upper arms, lifting her; she twisted free and staggered off the steps into Roseveare Court. Cold blotched her face. Her tawny-red eyes fixed on Bevil.

"I have bed news," rumbled the Lord-Architect. "Polly Calmady. He's to hang."

"H—?"

An aspirate too soft for speech.

"They re-arrested and tried him today. His boy here told me."

"It's true." Bevil's voice shook.

The woman giggled. Both hands clapped over her mouth, eyes bright. She snorted. She sprang back in a half-melted snowdrift, oblivious of cold; one hand out protectively: her bare flesh facing his suddenly drawn blade. "No, that's . . . it's not . . ."

"*You laugh!*"

"No, you . . . I had no warning—but you can't say they lied . . ."

She wiped a bare wrist across eyes that brimmed, water suddenly running down her cheeks, her mouth twisting. Twice on an outbreath she struggled for speech: mewed. Beside Bevil, Casaubon's immense bulked stilled, his forehead creasing.

"*—she—*"

The woman shivered. Her jaw rattled. Through shudders, all but unintelligible, she managed to say: "They just took her down when I got there."

Bevil stared. Casaubon's outstretched hand sank back to his side.

"I found out from the Tower where . . . Desire Guillaime. I never thought of her *living* anywhere, you know that? I never thought. I had a talisman-cure for her illness, I thought I would go and talk with her on my way back, settle some things, I don't know."

One of her barleyrow braids, unravelling, stroked her chin
with wet tendrils of hair. Melted snow dripped from her
cloak.

"They saw I was a Master-Physician so the old woman
called me in. They'd taken her down and wrapped her in
blankets and warmed bricks, but she was dead. In her room
at St. Sophia. She hanged herself. She left me—"

Her head went back. She laughed, breathless, great gouts
of mist jerking out into the cold night; and the laughter
echoing off wood-and-plaster shop fronts. Tears stood in her
eyes.

Now her voice never wavered from its high, strained
pitch:

"She left Valentine Roseveare a letter. I didn't own to it.
When I left, the old woman *thanked* me."

X

$\mathbf{M}$uffled church bells rang. Valentine White Crow scratched through tangled hair and caught up the trailing edge of her nightrobe. Bed's warmth clung. The bright-haired baby, half-asleep in the crook of her arm, nuzzled at her shoulder; and she put her free hand across the child's back, nudging the sixth-floor bedroom door open with her foot. The sounds of Casaubon's dressing came from the floor below.

For the first time in five days, she focussed.

"About, are you?" A dark head appeared in the stairwell: Abiathar with a tray. "This is late. Sorry. I've had a kitchen full of runagate mercenaries since five this morning."

Snow-light spiked her puffy eyes. "Mercenaries?"

"Wanting to talk to your husband."

White Crow took the tray one-handed. A few rashers coiled on a tin plate, and a mug of half-warm tea slopped. Hunger suddenly growled in her gut.

"What day is it?"

"Wednesday."

"I think I . . . slept a lot." She hitched her elbow, offering the baby, and the black-haired woman came forward and cradled the child in her arms.

"Will you let me feed her now, then? I thought you were never going to let go of her."

"I needed comfort. Jadis lets me talk to her. And doesn't say anything." Both hands to the tray now, standing in the chill, bright hall; her feet cold on the floorboards. She strained her hearing. Far below, resonating up the stairwell, the sharp notes of a harpsichord sounded.

"Wednesday?"

The woman nodded curtly, vanishing down the stairs. "A fine day for a hanging-match."

Snow and harpsichord music: both sharp, alert.

She set the tray down inside the bedroom door, scratching at her breasts under her nightgown and smelling the frowstiness of five days a-bed. The merry music spiked behind her eyes.

Eating one-handed as she crossed and recrossed the room, the woman threw on long hose under knee-breeches, short knee-hose, two shirts against the cold, and the leather doublet over all. She finished the last of the tea standing, hooking one foot and then the other into shoes; banged the cup down on the tin tray, and took the stairs at a run going down.

Abiathar twisted her dyed-black hair around her fingers, pinning it back with polished bone pins. "Is all set?"

"Ed Kitterage is back in the stables, with a musket. Damned if he don't freeze before this lot finish. I'll keep watch upstairs." Hazelrigg spat on the sawdust floor. "You'll watch here?"

Abiathar nodded. "It's left to us to protect the children. She must always have been foolish. Why else would she have been thrown out of Roseveare to begin with?"

"Who knows what she'll do now? Wish I were back home."

"You be careful with the little one, Thomas."

The short dark man grunted. Jadis, in the crook of his

arm, grabbed at the gloved fingers that he offered. Thomas Hazelrigg held out his hand for the feeding-bottle.

"She—"

A burst of loud laughter outside the kitchen parlour drowned out speech. Abiathar went to the door. A thin, curly-haired mercenary in pink satin leaned over the ground-floor bannisters. Slush and a searing-cold wind blew in from the front door.

"Have a jug of mulled wine sent up, while we wait on your master. Quick now, woman!"

"Sir." She measured her tone just short of contempt.

"Half of 'em well drunken, and it's only nine of the clock." Hazelrigg teased the bottle-teat around the child's lips until she fastened herself determinedly and began to suck. He eased back in the wing-armed kitchen chair. Glowing brown eyes met Abiathar's. He chuckled. "Not one of 'em sober to watch their Captain hang!"

"Let him hang. He didn't kill her, but he might have, so let him hang." The black-haired woman set wine to heat on the kitchen-range, that stank of sea-coal and pine kindling. "Or they can hang *her*. They killed the girl between them. She'd have welcomed it any time these five days."

The White Crow hit the last stair, swung round into the landing, and stopped. For thirty seconds she stood still, her expression blank. Small noises of occupation came from behind the closed door. She raised her fist, rapped a sharp tattoo, and entered on the rumble of "Come!"

"Hello."

She walked forward. Blankets slumped from the bed to the rugs, showing where the fat man had risen. He sat silhouetted against the windows at the room's far end, head resting on one fist, staring down at the snow-covered yard and stables entrance. One brow raised as he registered her entrance.

"Breakfast!" She reached across his shoulder, filching a

pork chop, and ripped off small bites of the meat, resting
her back up against the window-shutter. Indistinctly, she
said, "You?"

"I'm not hungry."

"The age of miracles!"

She threw the half-eaten chop back on the plate. A coal
fire hissed in this bedroom's grate, whistling softly with the
escape of gasses. Cold at her back, the leaded windows
began to mist with the heat of her body. The White Crow
chewed and wiped her wrist across her greasy mouth.

The Lord-Architect's chins rested on his plump hand,
drowned in the lace-fall at his cuff. Waistcoat and breeches
remained unbuttoned, his shirt-tail hanging into his lap. One
garter fixed up a stocking, the other wrinkled about his
ankles. He raised his eyes.

"I know. I'm sorry." She swallowed the chewed lump of
tough meat, wincing. "I shut myself away from everybody,
not just you."

"Liar."

The equable friendliness of his tone made her flinch.
Turning, she rubbed a clear space in the window's frost,
staring down at Kitterage as he led another gentleman-mercenary's horse into the stables.

"I forced her. As much as *he* did. I really did." She wiped
her fingers down her breeches. "I'd sooner have slept and
forgotten this day, I think. If it were over, I'd know what I
felt."

Her finger traced patterns on the glass: uncompleted sigils
of power, of planetary *numina: Claviclulae* from ancient gri-
moires, and the Signatures of hedgerow herbs. The wet glass
chilled her flesh. She expunged the patterns with the heel
of her hand. His gaze prickled the hairs on the back of her
neck.

"Is she buried yet?"

"St. Giles Cripplegate. Here . . ."

Some apprehension twisted in her bowels. The White

Crow put her hands in her pockets and turned, coming no closer to the seated man. He dug his plump hand into a waistcoat pocket and drew out a folded, stained sheet of paper.

"Here."

"I don't want it."

Hands on chair-arms, he pushed himself up lightly and quickly; blinking at her against the window's snow-light. One fat hand flourished impatiently in her face. "Read it!"

"Who brought it here?"

A pause: she snatched the paper from his hand, crumpling it into a ball in her fist, and threw herself down into the opposite seat. She helped herself to acorn-coffee from the jug, drinking from Casaubon's cup, making a face at how cold and sour it tasted. "Well?"

"The grandmother. Rot it, she could find *Roseveare* easily enough! If it eases you, she knows nothing to put Roseveare and a Master-Physician into her mind together."

"No one knows. I'd almost rather they were making broadsheet ballads about it."

Without opening her fist, the White Crow rested her mouth against her fingers. Tears thickened in her throat. She blinked rapidly. She dropped the crumpled ball of paper on the table, smoothing it down against the wood. A thin line in black ink superscribed it *Valentine of Roseveare*. She turned it over.

"The seal's broken—you've opened this!"

The Lord-Architect Casaubon hitched up black woollen breeches, abandoned the two top buttons as impossible, and shrugged his waistcoat across his mountainous stomach. He scratched through his copper-red hair. Blue eyes fixed on her.

"Of *course* I've read it. What do you think I am? Would I give it to you unread?"

"I never think, do I?"

She put her feet up on the table, booted ankles crossed.

The crumpled paper rested in her lap. Outside, a lump of snow fell without warning from gutter to yard. Dawn dulled from acid-white to grey.

"Are you going to see him?" She snorted, shook her head. "See you, I don't even know—have you seen him these five days?"

The Lord-Architect finished buttoning his waistcoat, head bent to the task, hair falling over his forehead. He straightened: not only a fat man, but a very large man also fat; blocking the window's light.

"If he doesn't hang for this, he'll hang for another rape. Or theft, or murder over a card-table. In two years or ten." His voice rumbled. "You'd have him hanged, not pardoned."

She tilted her head against the chair's back. Snow-light gleamed in the ceiling's ornamental plaster strapwork. Winding patterns with no detectable cause or ending. She pulled a strand of white-streaked red hair to her mouth and sucked on it.

"He raped her. She's dead. Somebody ought to suffer for that. I . . . perhaps it should be me."

"Read your damned letter. I'm leaving the house this half-hour."

She touched the paper with a fingertip.

"What does it feel like, to write and be knowing all the time that you're going to kill yourself? Do you even believe it, do you think? These past five days I've expected her to walk in . . . and I *touched* her, I know how cold her body was."

The Lord-Architect moved. The back of his hand rested against her cheek, and the White Crow leaned her head a little to that side, breathing in the scent of soap and new linen.

"I don't understand why she did it. I know it was my fault but I really, really, don't know why."

A plump knuckle rapped her ear, too light to be a cuff. The White Crow took the letter up from her lap and flipped it open: thrice-folded, marked with fingerprints, torn down one edge, and the writing clear and uneven and without a blot:

Madam I understand now why you abused me the cause of it being my sickness which will be my death, so i will prevent by going first. I had begun to think of some affection from yr. self but now is much changed. You wd. not tell me my flesh is corrupted, is this your mark of affection?

Madam it was in my mind to pray you suffer as I do but the prayers of the corrupt in heart make no breach in heaven. I am become abomination. Or man or woman, they scent it out and come to me. If not before, then by this.

Guillaime

A coal popped in the grate. She moved her shoulders as one does unconsciously in sub-zero temperatures, tense against the shrinking of flesh.

"*What* sickness?"

She slammed the letter down on the table, springing up; standing over Casaubon where he sat on the bed, legs apart, fumbling between them on the floor for a stout shoe.

"Rot it, what sickness do you think? I went to the local priest-surgeon in St. Sophia. Who else'd fill her head with damnation for the sake of a mild dose of pox?" The Lord-Architect sat up. Either exertion or anger reddened his face. "He'd seen her two hours before she died. All righteous indignation and piety when I hammered his door down—*he* welcomed her death."

The White Crow pressed a fist into her stomach, just under the arch of her ribs. Sweat chilled her. She snuffled a small laugh, shaking her head, blinking eyes rubbed sand-raw with weeping and now dry.

" '*I had begun to think of some affection from yourself.*' "

Her fingers scrabbled across the oak, reaching to seize the

letter from the table again. " *You would not tell me my flesh is corrupted'*—oh, sweet Jesus. Oh, lord."

Tears spilled down her face. She pushed a wet hand across her cheek. The Lord-Architect bent his head, hooking on his shoe with one plump finger. She slumped down on the bed beside him and leaned against his solid arm and shoulder.

"You went there? Was it safe not to be jealous when she was dead?"

"Valentine!"

"The truth is always appalling. No—I don't do you justice. You meant to protect me, to find out the truth of this."

She slowly folded the letter and put it in her doublet's inside pocket.

"Will you stop telling me what I did and didn't mean!" Casaubon trod his heel down into the buckled black shoe and stood. "For my part I'd as soon she was alive and you with a chance to tire of her."

"I didn't know she was so vulnerable."

"Rot it, she's dead, there's an end to it."

Roseveare House echoed to footsteps, calls. The clamour sounded louder from lower floors. The Lord-Architect reached up for his coat, laid it across the back of the chair, took two pistols from the pockets, and checked their priming before stowing them away again.

"Young Bevil will have me to go Whitehall again and plead a pardon." He looked delicately at her. "What will you do?"

"When does the man go to Tyburn?"

"Between two and three."

"I'll meet you here before then." She touched her doublet. Paper crackled. "I have somewhere to go, first."

The hired coach slowed and stopped. Jared leaned forward and peered between the blind and the window. A white world glowed: early morning.

"You wait here, Jarrie."

The coach-door swung open. Wet, cold air blasted in. Jared drew his knees together and put his gloved hands on them. Plumes of white breath feathered away from him. He leaned back against the worn upholstery as his mother stepped down into the snow. His throat constricted.

The coach stood high enough for him to see over the wall of St. Giles Cripplegate, into the churchyard. Heaps of tarpaulin-covered planks lay chalked with snow, the planks covering holes already dug before winter hardened the ground.

At the end of the row, raw earth stood proud of the snow in a long hump. Jared pulled the blind aside and stared down at the grave. His mother stood in the snow in front of it with her head down.

She squatted, suddenly, the folds of her leather cloak crumpling on the ground. One of her fists punched the earth's soft-looking new ridges. She lifted her knuckles to her mouth and sucked grazes.

Her footprints would be deep in the snow if she walked farther away from the coach.

He kicked rhythmically at the opposite seat. A splinter of wood sprang loose. He hooked the toe of his boot under it, worrying at it, sliding down in his seat until he lay almost flat. The cold air made his uncovered ears burn.

Deep footprints leading away, never returning.

The coach door opened.

His mother swung herself lightly up, not bothering with the let-down steps. Her face shone red, shiny. Jared stood up as the coach jolted off and stumbled between her knees to put his arms around her neck. Cold air clung to her hair, smelling of ice and damp earth.

"Is that where the lady's dead?"

"I'll watch him hang and be glad of it." Her voice buzzed beside his ear. She moved her head back. A moving strap of light, between blind and coach-window, striped her face and the shoulder of her cloak. His hands hurt where she gripped them.

"It wasn't *just* me, baby. It was him as well."

Jared staggered as the coach cornered. He sat half on and half against her knee. "I'm glad she's dead! She made you unhappy."

"Jarrie, for the Lord's sake—!"

He reached up and touched the cinnamon-red braids, streaked with white; and let his fingers move to that most favorite familiar mystery, the tiny, soft pin-feathers clustered at her temples.

"I love you. I hate everybody who makes you sad."

Skin around her eyes crinkled, as if the shifting sunlight blinded. "My commendable son."

"What's 'commendable'?"

She hugged him hard, one arm about his shoulder. The coach jolted.

"If I had to go on a long journey, pudding, would you come with me?"

He leaned against her breast, kicking one foot against her boot. "But will papa come?"

Still and silent for a heartbeat, she traced his cheek with her knuckle.

"You're going to have to wait in the coach again. I have one more place to visit before I take you home."

Freezing damp breathed from the walls.

She walked swiftly down one side of Pit Ward. Wet straw rustled underfoot. Water running down from the high, barred windows congealed into ice. Men and women in worn clothes huddled in the straw. Coughs racked the air: prison-fever.

The cold struck up through the soles of her boots. One elbow on her purse, her hand near her dagger, the White Crow shoved through the crowd of prisoners and turnkeys. Steps ascended under a masonry arch to the Masters Ward.

The centre of each tread bowed, stone worn down a good five-fingers' depth.

She pressed a silver penny into the hand of a leather-coated guard, ducked under his halberd, and ran up the steps two at a time. The pile of papers under her arm slipped and she grabbed at it, showing her teeth in a fierce grin; paid another penny to the guard at the head of the stairs, and halted in the archway. She stretched one hand out to the iron-studded oak door for support.

Two or three dozen groups of ill-dressed men and women clustered in the hall. Light from half-hooped windows slanted down, barred, upon battered old tables at which prisoners and their visitors drank and played dice. A few tiny braziers glowed with coals. The raucous noise hesitated a second, summed up and ignored her. The White Crow narrowed her eyes.

A cold and acid pain seared in her stomach; her lungs struggled for air. The straw tangled her boots as she walked towards one window embrasure.

His scarlet frock-coat covered the granite, spread across the ledge under the window. He sat on it in a filthy shirt and breeches, leaning forward, the curls of his periwig crushed and stuck with straw; and all the strength of muscular arm and back engaged in stillness.

Pollexfen Calmady placed a greasy playing-card on top of a third, removed his hands with swift care. The card-tower trembled and stood. Five storeys high. She with one wrist-movement skimmed a handful of pamphlets into the cards, knocking all into the air. The man jumped to his feet. He stood barefoot, leg-irons around his ankles.

"There."

The stone wall slammed against her shoulderblades as she threw herself down to sit on the stone. She stared up. He slowly pulled up his coat and draped it around his shoulders. She bent and picked some pamphlets from the floor, flipping the Ace of Spades off a title page.

"*Captain Calmady's Last and Dying Speech, a Gallows Recantation.* And *The Ballad of a Gentleman-Murderer.* I like that. And more. There are hawkers selling dozens of titles outside the prison gate."

Pollexfen Calmady sat down facing her at the far end of the window embrasure. His red-knuckled hand moved to separate the pamphlets. Chilblains whitened two of his fingers.

"*Confession at the Tyburn-Mare, or, The Ravisher Undone to Public View.*" Taunting, she let every syllable sound; mocking the gentleman-mercenaries' mannered tone. She reached up and tugged her cloak-tie open, struggling for breath. "Do you like it, Captain Calmady? Will you say anything as good, do you think, before you dance on air?"

The big man shrugged his arms into his coat-sleeves. "I suppose, as they say, I'll piss when I can't whistle. So it's seen: *plures crapula quam gladius*, drunkenness kills more than the sword."

Morning sun fell on her cheek from the barred window. Almost warm. The stench of urine, excrement, smoke, and sour wine made her cough. She rubbed at the corner of one wet eye. The stone's cold sank into her back and thighs.

The White Crow stared.

Something loosened in her chest at the sight of him: the dirt-marked and ripped scarlet breeches and coat, and the battered periwig. His sword-belt hung, the hanger empty. The creases in his face deepened, by shadow or by starvation, and he snapped his fingers and looked aside, and took a tin jug from one of the ragged children running errands.

"I might have known Gadsbury or Lacey would pay to have you in the best Ward. Or is it my Casaubon's money?"

"Will you drink with me?"

She backhanded the jug, knuckles stinging. Brackish water splashed the straw. Her cloak slipped down. She lurched forward, fisting both hands in the shirt and lace at his neck, fingers digging into his flesh; knocked his head back against the wall and spat.

Spittle dripped down his eye, cheek, and lip.

"No, I will *not* drink with you. She's dead because of you."

His brilliant dark eyes blinked. Not touching her, his hand

moved to feel the back of his head, the blow somewhat softened by his long, curling wig. One foot on the floor and one on the stone window-seat, she let the knowledge of his strength and her unused, unhandy knife show on her face, and grinned, and in the middle of it sat back heavily and caught her breath in the middle of a laugh.

"I know she's dead. I have learned to think on it, here." He wiped his sleeve across his face. "No act of mine, but I look on this day as my atonement for it."

"*Atonement?*"

"You revile me rightly. I killed the girl as surely as if these two hands hanged her. And your two hands." The man's head lifted. "As surely as if you knotted the halter."

Blood beat in her ears, and her heart's fibrillation shook her breathless. She slowly stood up. The light glinted in his eyes, with that manic brightness either humour or despair; subtly altered now.

"What can you keep from servants? One hears all from them." His shoulders moved under the torn coat. His skin glowed yellow, waxy; and his teeth showed stained. Foul breath drifted across the intervening space. "Madam, whatever passed between you and her, I am responsible. I am *glad* of this day. Now I would not have it otherwise."

"Oh, *surely.*"

She reached to touch his hand. Flesh, cold with stone-fever and shock. She stepped back. A rat scuttled over her boots, and she kicked it absently and instantly against the wall; its fragile skull crushed.

"No doubt—" He got heavily to his feet, the striped sunlight cruelly illuminating his ripped clothes and dirt. "—No doubt others will visit me today, but I have this, now, to say to you."

Pollexfen Calmady knelt, in wet straw and on cold stone, on both knees.

"For any offence I may have done you or led you into, forgive me."

She stared, appalled. "This is too serious for—"

And continued to stare, wordless. He lifted his head,
meeting her eyes.

"Valentine?"

Her feet moved her away, hands making small, unconscious gestures of disassociation. "You weren't so unconscious of your offence as you pretended, or else you couldn't
have performed it!"

"You're not Guillaime, madam. It's you I ask."

She looked down at her hands. They shook. She held
them out, closing his scarred fingers in her palms; half-said
a word, nodded, lifted her wrists so that he must stand, his
hands still in her grasp.

"What did you ever do to her that I didn't do?" She let
go, her hands clasping together. He looked down, his face
dazzled. Her voice sharpened. "Was yours an honest error?
Mine wasn't. I knew she trusted a physician and I used that,
and I didn't even *think* about not doing it."

His hand lifted. She flinched. His fingers touched the pin-
feathers at her temples, a touch as light as Jared's. She
caught a sob in her throat and choked, stammered out,
"Damn you, I didn't know to tell her; I didn't know she'd
go to some Protectorate fanatic; I didn't know she *believed*—"

She wiped her nose on her sleeve.

"Damn, you gave it her."

He rested one fist back on his hip, unconsciously showing
the rent lining of his long coat. The lines deepened in his
face. He smiled a slow smile. "Madam, you and I are, *ipso
facto*, too alike for you ever to forgive me."

"Alike?"

She took a breath, deep despite the stink of damp and
excrement, held it, and let it out in a long sigh. Anger
dissipated; she raked at it without result.

"That's true, of course. I've seen it for some while."

He inclined his head. The periwig, dusty on one side,
shone in the window's light. One chilblained finger stabbed
the air at her. "Will you hear me advise you somewhat?
Purely for yourself, and because I will shortly have to speak

truth about greater matters, and may as well begin to
practise."

She nodded silently.

"You use your *magia* less and less."

The dislocation disorientated her. She grinned without
humour. "After this, I won't use it at all; I can't be a physician now!"

"You never could. This is not your husband telling tales,
madam; I have eyes and ears—let me guess. You left the
road and put up your sword, and since then have done less
and less of the Noble Arts, until now you do almost nothing
but doctor servant's influenzas and children's green-bone
fractures."

Precision and control informed him; she could only look.

"How do you know? And what's it to you?"

"I'm a dying man." He spoke with undramatic sobriety.
"One of the things I have thought of, these five days, is you.
I know you as I know myself. *Find yourself a war*—if you
wait until spring, or summer, the damned bitches will pro-
vide a civil war here between 'em, but you'd fare better
fighting strangers. *Fight.* Aren't half the Invisible College
scholars and soldiers, as you were?"

"Oh, how can I?" She rubbed her hands over her face,
fingers rough against brows and hairline. "I'm a Master-
Physician, I heal wounds, I don't make them. I *can't* do the
magia that I used. Well then: I can't."

A ragged girl of seven or eight shoved between them.
Pollexfen Calmady leaned down and picked up the tin jug
and tossed it to her. The child ran off. He beat dirt off the
fabric of his knee-breeches and straightened.

"Admirable sentiments. Yes, and what I recommend is a
worse way. But answer me: is it in your nature? You do
violence to yourself, being what you try to be here. I say
nothing in defence of fighting, except that you'll sicken as
long as you don't carry a blade and use it. Oh, believe it,
wars are pig-butchery and stink and no honour; *I* know!
Madam, I beg you ask yourself if you can do anything *else*."

"I don't—I'm not—"

A handbell clanged at the far end of the Ward. His head turned.

"I should be glad of your company now."

"What is it?"

"The service for the condemned. I doubt my damned fool troopers will be here until later. But this is appointed my day to die. I welcome it."

"Do you?"

"Were it vice versa, say, how would you stand?"

The White Crow looked away. Warders pushed through the crowds of prisoners and visitors, sorting out candidates for the service. The noise-level rose. She rescued her cloak from the straw and put it about her shoulders, shivering.

"Will you do something for me, madam?"

With no hesitation she nodded.

"I have no more money. Everything in this rotten hell-hole must be paid for, light and air included. Well," Pollex-fen Calmady said, "Gadsbury and the rest have no money, either. Will you tell Casaubon, either I must sell my dead body to the surgeons, or else hang in rags. Tell him I won't hang without a clean shirt and stockings to die in."

A tall turnkey grabbed his arm and he shrugged her off, turning to follow nonetheless; shouting back over his shoulder: "Will you tell him?"

"I . . . *yes.*"

She elbowed her way in his wake. A woman with a musket barged past; two black-jerkined halberd men at the far door jostled. She dropped a hand to her belt, found her purse gone; walking with numb legs until she knelt on the chapel's stone floor.

White granite gleamed.

The squat round pillars shone, dappled with yellow-and-gold from the stained-glass perpendicular windows. A dozen or so prisoners knelt and their warders with them. The child-priest Ordinary of Newgate strode up the aisle, black robe whisking into her face as he passed. The cold stone hurt her knees. She lifted her head.

Carved deep into the blank eastern wall, Square and Star shone with inlaid brass. In the center the Circle blazed, polished by unwilling hands; enclosing the image of the Risen Sun. She drew the sign of Bull-horns on her breast, consciously resuscitating childhood practises.

Pollexfen Calmady and one other condemned man knelt at what at first seemed a low wooden table, set below the wall's bas-reliefs. Under his wig, his face showed white, calm, poised.

Abruptly a bell rang out, tolling harshly in Newgate's tiny chapel tower.

Split pine planks wept pungent scent into the air. She craned her head. The heads of new copper nails glinted in the open wooden coffin.

XI

Jared shivered after the long wait. His mother eased down in the coach-seat, digging into a concealed pocket. She counted a handful of pennies, half-pence, farthings, and extracted one remaining rose-noble.

"Give this to the coachman when he leaves you at Roseveare House."

Jared folded his hand around the coin. The septagon's edges dug into his palm. "What about you, mama?"

"Looks like I'll have to walk."

She flashed a smile that, from warm eyes and wry mouth, reached in and tugged his gut. He clung to her for a kiss.

"Don't worry! Tell your father I'll be back before noon. And I will be, pudding."

The coach-door opened: shut. Tack jingled. The coach's wheels rachetted on gravelled snow, skidding and then gripping. One of the leaders neighed. Jared jerked the blind and it rolled up.

Tiny between the grandeur of stone lions and frozen fountains, the woman walked fast, shoes skidding, towards Whitehall.

*   *   *

"What do you mean, she won't see me?" The White Crow glared at the elderly lady-in-waiting. "She damned well *will* see—Denzil!"

Sir Denzil Waldegrave walked through the courtyard from the Banqueting Hall to Whitehall Palace's east wing. His amber cane poked delicately at the gritted cobbles. The wind moved the long, golden curls of his wig, and the azure ribbons at cuffs and cane.

"*Sir* Denzil." She abandoned the woman and loped across the yard, pushing between Protectorate guards and royalist courtiers to lay a hand on the man's arm. "I need to see Her Majesty."

His leisurely stride never altered.

"Dammit!"

"Lady Roseveare—"

The mid-morning sun gleamed from the dyed-gold horse-hair curls of his wig, and made his rouged cheeks into a clown's garish mask. From this, shrewd brown eyes surveyed her.

"—I can't conceive your business here. If it be for yourself, abandon hope. If for a friend, let your friend find some other advocate." He paused to kick horse-dung from the heel of his court shoe, speaking in a measured undertone. "The gratitude of monarchs is, never to forgive a favour. You have been of use. You have affronted her dignity. She has said that if she lays eyes on you again, she will send you to Newgate or the Tower. Be warned."

The White Crow stared.

"Truly?"

"Send in to know as many times as you please. But expect her in due course to send out a sergeant-at-arms." He extracted a watch from his waistcoat pocket, flipped up the silver lid, and in louder tones remarked, "Five-and-twenty to eleven, an it please your ladyship."

"This isn't for me."

"Then, whoever's cause it is, your name will do them more harm than help. Madam, I beg you to excuse me."

She slowed, elbowed by passers-by, staring after the man,
buffeted aside. Sun glinted from the rows of windows. Ice
hung jagged from gables, six-foot spears that could fall and
impale a man. The cold wind sank bone-deep into her body.

The grave, not yet sunken, scars yesterday's snow. Frozen
clods of its earth are rimed with white. No headstone. A
pauper's grave.

Bevil Calmady absently fingers a hole in his blue silk
waistcoat. His thick scarlet coat, hanging open, could wrap
his thin torso two or three times. It is not his. He reaches
up and removes his hat.

The broken plume annoys him; he snaps it off.

Whispering, "I apologise for him," he feels in his pocket
for the crackling paper that, signed, will apprentice him to
Captain Huizinga's surgeon (a Paracelsan of limited temper
and great skill) for seven years. He adds, "I apologise for
them all."

St. Giles Cripplegate looms, cold black stone. The dragon-
weathervane squeals, shifting to south-south-east, and cries
in brazen tongues:

"Eleven o'clock and all's well! Eleven o'clock and aaaak—"

Bevil Calmady lowers his arm from a stoop and throw that
is all one movement. The stone from Desire Guillaime's
grave rebounds and rattles down the church tiles.

Sand melted old snow to the colour of excrement, a sick
yellow on the cobblestones. Grit crunched under her boots.

The White Crow elbowed between groups of people
crowding the bottom of the Charing Cross Road. Virgin
white on the gables of shops, snow stood out against a sunny
sky. Wind gusted coldly.

Her stomach growled with the smell of new-baked bread.
She slowed under the white plaster and black-beamed over-
hang of the nearest shop.

A shape moved behind the irregular glass shop-window;
pushing open the door to the street. The Lord-Architect

tilted his head back, bit into a pastry, and caught sight of her.

"Valentine!"

A spray of crumbs dotted the slush and her cloak. She brushed herself off thoughtfully.

"I want—" She put a last fragment of pastry in her mouth, chewed, and raised her eyebrows. "I need to talk to you."

The wind blew tendrils of copper-red hair across his forehead. Cold reddened his faintly freckled face. A scarf muffled his chins; the green frieze coat's hem showed black with wet; snow and muck covered his large boots. Passers-by divided like a river to go into the road and around him.

"Any time these five days you could have talked to me." The syrup pastry broke in his hand. He held up his large, dripping fingers and licked them.

"I know. I'm sorry."

The Lord-Architect Casaubon probed with his tongue between ring and little finger, gave up on the last fragment, and brushed absently at the flakes of pastry around his lips and chin. His blue eyes glanced north towards the turn-off into Roseveare Court.

"Here."

He pushed the shop-door open again, bowed to an elderly man leaving with arms full of loaves, and shifted himself sideways to climb crabwise up narrow stairs towards the first floor, not looking back to see if she followed.

At the head of the stairs, private coffee-rooms opened off the landing. She beat her hands against the warmth of returning circulation and walked into the front room. A fire burned in the hearth. Bottle-glass windows looked down into the crowded streets. The fat man sprawled across one complete side of the oak-panelled cubicle nearest the window.

"I hope you can buy me coffee." She sat heavily on the opposite side. "I don't have any money left. You know how much it costs in petty bribes in Newgate."

His copper-red brow hooked up. "You've spoken to him?"

"I've spoken to him."

"And?"

A leather-aproned man put his head around the door. The Lord-Architect Casaubon listed rapidly: "Coffee, dates, pork chop, steak; what sweetmeats you have; the coffee with cream if you have it fresh."

"Sorry, master." The man shrugged. "Lot a custom on a hanging-day; always is. Take your coffee black, will you?"

"Black and without interruption."

The White Crow sneaked a sight of the coin handed over: too large to be a rose-noble, more probably a sovereign. She leaned her chin on her hand, staring through distorting window-glass into the street.

The door clicked shut.

"And?"

"And—he has me forgetting that it was he who broke into a sick woman's room and raped her while she was unconscious. And forgetting that he gave her the pox when he fucked her. And that she died as a direct result of what he did."

She sat back on the settle, burying her chin in the small ruffles at her neck.

"And forgetting that on campaign he wouldn't think twice about it. How many little girls has he fucked or killed, do you think, in forty years?"

"Fewer than you imagine." Casaubon's voice rumbled. "I won't call him innocent of what you say."

"Innocent!"

Sickness roiled under her breastbone.

"And yet there's the reason why I forget. Because he does want to die. He's content. It makes me wonder what I should be?"

Casaubon snorted. His distorted reflection in the window scowled. She shrugged.

"How am I different from him? Shall I hang myself, all three? Wouldn't that make a tragedy for Master Kinsayder's theatre. Casaubon, what can I do?"

His tone came very drily. "Little one, you can stop being ridiculous."

She felt her cheeks heat. "So I'm not about to hang myself. I won't say it doesn't have its temptations. I won't go to a man's hanging when I feel as guilty as he is."

The fire's heat soaked through her damp breeches. She slid sideways on the padded seat and pulled off first one shoe and then the other, and massaged her sweat-dark hose. Exhaustion burned sweetly in her muscles. Brief sleep pulled at her eyelids. The door slammed open, the coffee-house owner carrying a tray; and she sat with her eyes shut and listened to his loading down the table. Hunger tipped into sudden revulsion with the smell of cooked meat.

She opened her eyes, poured out coffee into chipped china, and sipped at the too-hot liquid. The Lord-Architect prodded his heaped plate with a fork. With her free hand she reached across and snared his deep cuff.

"And you? What will you do?"

He brandished a fork dripping gravy from the chop.

"Rot the man, if *I* hadn't written, he'd be here in town still, and the Guillaime girl alive."

"You're angry. And not just with me. Where did you go this morning?"

She felt down the cuff to his other hand, winding her fingers between his; resting their joined hands against her cheek. His voice, more vibration than sound, came quietly to her:

"To General Olivia. She claims no more say in the matter. Then I went to your Carola and she refused point-blank to see the General's renegade architect. The man was my friend. Guillaime never was, nor," his blue eyes met hers, "was ever likely to be."

The White Crow frowned.

"Something else?" she asked.

He pulled his hand from hers. Her skin suddenly chilled, she tucked her fingers up into her armpit, in the warmth of cloak and doublet. He planted one plump finger on his steak and sawed at it with the blunt knife.

"I'm wondering—" he rested the knife, picked up the steak and bit it, and continued through a mouthful of fibres and gravy "—how you contrive to be so comprehensive a fool."

"Me?"

"I will bear with you when you must come home to this commonwealth, it being your home; and I'll even bear with you when you fall for a pretty little face—and the idea that there's more brains than fanaticism behind it."

He picked out a string of gristle from between his teeth and dropped it. It lodged in the wrinkles of his unbuttoned coat. He prodded the air in her direction with the fork.

"But when you go off into the sulks, and lock yourself away with that bawling brat of mine: *no*. When you claim to be the Invisible College's physician-magus and confine yourself to doctoring influenza and greenstick fractures: *no*— what did I say?"

Tears started in her eyes. The coffee burned her upper lip. She sniffed and took a deeper drink. "Nothing."

"I'll stand no more."

He stuck a forefinger into his coffee-bowl, winced, drank it straight down and poured another, his cheeks reddening. She blinked. Sudden sunlight whitely illuminated the swell of his chest, the half-undone lace stock at his throat, and the delicate flesh of his throat, chins, and earlobes.

"I'm not your refuge to come home to when all else's exhausted!"

"No, I—yes," the White Crow said. "Yes, I did think . . . not to say *think*, but assume. Oh, damn you."

He reached across and cupped her cheek with gravy-smeared fingers. "Great Architect, but you're *white*."

"Only in places." Her voice wavered on the caustic tones. She sat back and smudged at her cheek with her sleeve. The sunlight brightened, leeching colour from the room; the crackle of the fire sounded loud in her ears.

Breathing slowed: she leaned her head back against the oak headboard.

"You're not glad I'm back then?"

The large man stopped with a coffee bowl halfway to his mouth. He put it down as delicately as if the chipped china had been porcelain.

Without raising her head, his eyes lifted to hers. "You might at least ask me whether I still want you."

She smiled, mouth closed, a fold of interior skin nipped between canine and lower tooth, biting against tears. At last, and aiming for sardonic superiority, she said, "I don't have to ask. I know. Which may be terrible, but is none the less true.".

The Lord-Architect Casaubon snorted.

One hand slammed down, palm flat on the table. Cutlery and cups jumped, spilled, rattled. His other hand grabbed her scholar's braids, pulling her up, half-standing over the wrecked table; he kissed her, and pushed gently. She hit the oak headboard partition between her shoulder-blades and sat down hard.

"Valentine. At least I've taught you *one* thing sufficiently well. Yes. *You know.* Now why did you ever forget it?"

Through the glass, the south-hanging sun warmed her cheek.

Fragile as ice, her composure started to return. She grinned, wiped her nose; and touched a finger to his. Sallow flesh against cherub-pink. She stared at his strong nail.

Grit-carts rumbled past in the street. Horses whickered.

"Did Jared tell you? I went to Whitehall Palace. Damn stupid thing to do; I ought to know *Regina* Carola by now."

"If you'd stood witness, it couldn't have been in his defence."

"I know that. You neither."

She picked desultorily at the edge of a pastry, staring out of the window. Cold condensation webbed the edges of the glass. Wavering images of men and horses passed below. Shadows slanted northwards.

"It must be close on midday." The Lord-Architect belched and got up from the alcove, scattering a handful of silver coin across his denuded plate.

She swivelled round and hurriedly pulled her boots on. "Now what?"

Casaubon, standing by the table, held open his lefthand coat pocket and tipped the dish of dates into it; and slipped the remains of the pork chop into his righthand pocket. He picked up the last jam pastry and bit into it.

"As to that—"

Crossing to the door, he cracked his head against a low beam and winced.

"—I have something more to tell you."

Outside, air dropped to freezing. The White Crow tugged on fur-lined leather gloves and stamped her feet. Gulls skimmed the roofs, skreeling north towards the river: flashes of white against the blue sky. Far down, past fountains and statues, the hundred chimneys of Whitehall Palace bled smoke into the midday haze.

The Lord-Architect, buttoning his coat, strode off up towards Roseveare Court. He spoke without looking at her and without slowing his pace.

"Did you know that Calmady raped the Guillaime woman twice?"

"*What?*"

"That first night that we got to town. I heard this about ten o'clock today, from Gadsbury and Bess Winslow. Rot it, the both of them are falling-down drunk; I think it's true."

"What the—?"

Breath sawed in her throat. She grabbed his arm as he wheeled into the road and heaved him back from the path of a carriage. In a niche between a saddlery shop and a milliners she let go of his coat-sleeve, shoving him back against the beamed wall.

"What do you mean, he raped her twice!"

Plumes of white breath spiralled into the air. She moved

from foot to cold foot, hugging herself, staring up at him. The fat man shook his head.

"The pair of whoreson bastards say he tracked her down to St. Sophia, threatened to tell her priest-confessor she was nothing but the mercenary company's whore; then had the two of them hold her down while he stripped her and lay with her, so that they could swear on oath to her nakedness. Her whorish nakedness."

She leaned forward against his chest, resting her forehead against the cold fabric of his coat. The rapid rise and fall of his breathing shook her. The weight of his arms around her shoulders pressed her to him, breath moistening the freize cloth.

A sedan-chair carrier elbowed her, passing. She straightened.

"That first night?'"

"I think so. This was two hours ago, Gadsbury so drunk he lay in his own piss and t'other no better; but yes, how else would they speak the truth?"

"Dear god. She couldn't tell me." Dazed, she stared up into his face. "He played young Bevil for a fool. Confessing and being arrested. He could *count* on her refusing to speak against him."

"That's all one now."

"Oh, sweet Christ!"

She reached up and linked her hands behind his neck. On her toes, breathing the cold wind, leaning up to kiss him on the corner of the mouth. "Christ, what a thing for you to hear. I wish I'd been with you."

He bent and rested his face in her neck, burrowing between ruff and braids; the warmth of his breath feathering her skin. She strained to encompass him in one embrace, slid back as he straightened up.

"What will you do?"

Casaubon shrugged massively. "I don't know yet. I make a beginning and tell you."

She linked her arm through his. The main bulk of the standing crowd left behind, she walked with him now between high brick frontages; the sun starring windows all down the road, hanging low in the southern sky and blinding her. Two horsemen spurred past. Clots of snow flew up, spattering her cloak.

"I . . ."

She stopped and stared back towards the square and Whitehall. "He knows me almost as well as you do. Pollex-fen Calmady."

Casaubon cocked his head, mutely questioning.

"He said we were alike. Him and me. Alike."

White haze blurred the far roofs. A keen wind blew up from the frozen Thamys. She hugged Casaubon's arm.

"Is that it? Do we just go home now?"

She frowned.

"And to Roseveare, in due course. Do we? If anything happens, it has to happen now: these next few hours."

"Rot it, don't say *we* when you mean *I*."

The White Crow winced. She narrowed her eyes against the winter sunlight, looking up at him.

She let go of his arm and stepped back, ankle-deep in slush at the roadside; pushing one thread of red hair back from her eyes. Voices called, chattered. Between hoofbeats and a distant sackbut, muffled church bells rang noon's thirteen chimes. The sun's warmth on her cheek felt a fragile thing.

She crossed her arms across her breast, gripping her upper arms.

"Will you . . ."

Not a smile: an upwelling of something too fierce and too joyous to be contained. She showed teeth. Her fingers dug deep into her biceps under the cloak. A deep breath: ". . . Will you trust me to do something, without my telling you?"

The Lord-Architect Casaubon raised his eyebrow, pained. "I most certainly will not."

"That's—fair."

"Do what you want," he said, "and count me with you, but not without knowing what it is. Credit me with some sense, furies take it!"

"Rein me and spur me, will you?" She laughed. Astonished, feeling it shake her body. She swung on her heel and strode towards Roseveare Court's back alley entrance, his shadow leaping ahead as he paced beside her.

No shifting hooves sounded in the stables, the gentlemen-mercenaries' mounts gone. Sun glinted from frost and cobbles. Seeing Abiathar, she snapped her fingers: the click echoing off yard walls.

The black-haired woman held the kitchen door open. "Shout next time. Kitterage might blow your head off. He's nervous."

The White Crow laughed. "*He's* nervous."

Abiathar and the Lord-Architect exchanged glances.

"Come with me. Both of you." She threw down her cloak and took the stairs from the kitchen parlour two at a time, heard the woman's questioning tone cut off as the door swung to; and made it as far as the second-floor front room before they caught up. She crossed to the desk and unlocked the drawer.

Casaubon, no sign of exertion in his face, unbuttoned his coat as he came into the room. Sunlight and warmth: and the smell of polished wood long neglected. She thrust the sheaf of folded papers into his hand.

"I'll sign these, unless you tell me I shouldn't."

In the far corner of the room an iron-banded long chest stood. She squatted and tried the key in the lock, wrist exerting force against the rust-starred metal.

"Damn, I—there!" She lifted her head.

The Lord-Architect stood in the centre of the room, head bent, reading. He handed each paper as he finished it to Abiathar. The woman wiped her hands on her skirts. She frowned in concentration, reading.

The White Crow opened the wooden chest.

A covering cloth. Parchments, rough against her hands as

autumn leaves, their inks faded into purples and sepias, but
the sigils still clear and strong. Two or three untitled books.
She stacked them reverently to one side on the floor. And
under it all, a mass of buckles, chains, leather straps, and a
scabbard.

"Deeds of property." The Lord-Architect folded the last
between two fingers and proffered it to Abiathar. She nodded acknowledgement.

"Abiathar, what say you?" The White Crow knelt up,
buckling the wide leather belt around her waist, over her
breeches-belt. Two rivetted chains hung down: one short,
one long. She clipped the one at her back to the lower
scabbard-clip, the one at her side to the clip closest the hilt,
and stood up.

And reached across with her left hand and drew the blade.

Oiled, cleaned, gleaming: no spot of rust. The razor edge
of a live blade. She touched a fingertip to it, near the point.
Burning as winter ice, a thin line of blood welled across the
pad of her finger.

"It's as near as I can get to a collective."

Abiathar cluckled sourly. "Try and deed property to servants and they'll have you in Bedlam, not Newgate."

The black-haired woman's eyes cleared. She tapped the
papers thoughtfully against her other hand. "I'll have to talk
to Thomas and Edward. I suppose we may answer for those
back at Roseveare? Now tell me if I have it right: you deed
us power of attorney, and all other necessary powers—" She
raised one script and read: "—for the maintenance of Roseveare Estate, its farms, properties, woods, and buildings; for
as long as the Roseveare family remain absent."

The sword's weight settled as the White Crow sheathed
it, tapping at mid-thigh, hilt ready for her hand. She met
Casaubon's gaze. Sober blue eyes watched, level.

"Absent for how long?" he asked.

"As long as you like."

The slight stress on the penultimate word brought a curve

to his delicately shaped mouth. He turned, took Abiathar's hand, and kissed it. "Count on no short absence!"

"Oh, I guessed as much, my lord."

The White Crow put both hands down to ease the sword-belt. At Casaubon's touch, she lifted her head. His finger caressed her cheek.

"You had this planned. Rot it, not because *I* want it?"

With a demure hilarity, she said, "Not just because you want it. There are others concerned."

"What about the children? Your son's no more than ten years from an age to inherit. And there's the child." Abiathar frowned. "I can promise you this, if either comes seeking Roseveare, they're as like to get a cold welcome as not."

"As far as I'm concerned, I'm giving you the place. They'll know it. It's up to you to keep it."

She snapped her fingers again, took the papers back and carried them to the desk, flipping open the inkwell and signing in scrawled quill-pen *Valentine Roseveare.*

"Now . . ."

Her boots clicked on the floorboards, pacing to the window. Roseveare Court's bookshops stood boarded up and left for the hanging-holiday. Snow choked all but a winding centre path. She squinted sideways, down between buildings towards the main road. Thoughts slotted into place, faster than words could follow.

"Bloody woman might have given the carriage back."

The Lord-Architect spluttered with laughter. She turned.

"*Well.* She didn't need that. Unless she plans to travel in it when she goes into exile, I suppose . . . We won't be able to leave town anyway until the weather shifts. Love, will you act the difficult part?"

Casaubon folded massive arms. She went on:

"Take Jared and the baby. This place will get ransacked, but that's no harm; they won't assume servants know where we've gone."

Abiathar, folding the signed documents, said, "Where will
you have gone?"

"I think . . ." She looked at the Lord-Architect,
prompting.

"The Liberty of Northbankside. One of the rooming-
houses there." He stooped to kiss Abiathar's cheek as the
older woman left the room. "Rot it, it *is* the worse part. I'll
do it provided I'm told all else. Now."

"I . . . have to do something about Pollexfen Calmady.
I've decided."

"Oh, good." The Lord-Architect beamed happily. "At
last."

She made the sort of laughter that is really exasperation,
one fist clenched, swinging round to point with her other
hand. The sword banged at her hip. "Don't you even *care*
if it's not moral—that it's the wrong thing to do?"

Casaubon continued to look at her, his immense body
still, the sun catching his copper hair and fair skin. Visible in
his face, finally, and visible to her: a ruthless benevolence.

The White Crow said, "For you it isn't even a question,
is it?"

He loomed over her; seized her under the arms and
pulled her up into an embrace, her feet eighteen inches
above the floor.

"You've made up your mind!" He kissed her
enthusiastically.

In the face of that massive refusal of judgement, she
sought interior certainties.

"So . . . it's the wrong decision, but it's mine, and I abide
by the consequences."

A single bell rang continuously, muffled, echoing down
through Newgate's stone walls. Pollexfen Calmady rested his
head back against the man's leather-aproned belly, stretching his throat and chin.

A razor feathered across his skin.

Prison ash-soap eased its passing. The last stubble scraped

away, he sat up and dabbed at his face with dirty shirt-sleeves. Gadsbury raised a slurred cheer. Arbella and Rule supported the small man; the tall woman leaning in turn on Bess, Lady Winslow, and the Margrave. The company of gentlemen-mercenaries crowded close, shouldering strangers further off. All the Pit muttered and buzzed with talk.

"Sir." Calmady rose and bowed to the man who shaved him.

"My pleasure, my master."

"Now strike off the chains."

Barred sunlight on the straw slanted north-east. Past two of the clock: the prison-yard outside a roar of gathering women and men and children. A shout went up at the rumble of wheels: the tumbril's arrival.

The brawny man acting as barber snapped his fingers. His hair and beard caught the light as he knelt, brass-blond; and he blinked slow, brandy-brown eyes. Two lads ran forward with mallet and chisel, a dozen younger brats at their heels. The man swept them back with a bare, muscular arm. He placed the chisel and raised the mallet.

Pollexfen Calmady, his back straight, looked down to his ankles. Iron chains coiled about his bare feet. The mallet lifted, fell. A rivet shot out, lost in filthy straw; one shackle sprang open. The reverberate echoes of the strike diminished in the vaulted hall.

Iron to anvil: smithy-noises. The second shackle fell loose.

"Again, sir, I thank you."

He walked a few paces, barefoot, straw pricking the soles of his feet; light at heel for the first time in five days, and ridiculously, momentarily, light at heart.

The fair-haired hangman's assistant rose. A leather apron covered black breeches and boots. His open face squinted against a bar of sunlight. Pollexfen Calmady pointed at a small man hovering behind him.

"You—you've a damned surgeon's look to you!"

The small man's eyes travelled up and down Calmady's thick torso. "Many a man has sold what he will shortly no

longer need to purchase what he would not be without. I'll
give you shillings enough to purchase clothes to be hanged
in."

Calmady locked eyes with the Margrave Linebaugh across
the man's head.

"See I'm given honest *untouched* burial. If not, I swear
you'll never ride without a dead man in the company!"

The Margrave lifted his arm slightly, weighed down with
folded shirt, breeches, and coat. "Your friend's servant
brought money, captain. And sends apologies that he dare
not attend."

Calmady snorted. "Has Baltazar Casaubon sense enough
to fear, now? That's a wonder!"

"You're a Queen's man, hanging; there'll be enough royalists there that the Protectorate's renegade architect might
well fear for his skin." Arbella Lacey held up polished white
boots. "He's done well by you, captain. As well as a man in
his position could."

He reached up between his shoulder-blades and pulled
the stinking shirt over his head. He did not look around,
nor look for missing faces. A hand held out a clean shirt, all
lace and linen, that slid over his skin, covering dirt and
prison-rash. He stripped breeches and stockings, received
new, and turned as he finished the fastenings.

"My god, will you look at that?" Lord Rule carefully re-
arranged one of the black periwig's curls on his captain's
brocade-coated shoulder. His gloved hand flicked across
white- and silver-lace splendour. "Flash. Very flash. We'll
have no cause to be shamed, knowing you today."

Pollexfen Calmady tugged boots on over white linen
breeches and stockings. The silver-laced waistcoat buttoned
a little tightly across his large chest. A momentary smile
moved his lips at that constriction. He shrugged into the
white brocade coat that Arbella held out, and put his fists
on his hips, staring down the Ward: at men lying drunk or
feverish against the walls, rats running across them; at a

bare-breasted slut suckling a child; at the faces all drawn to follow him.

"I'm a magnetic north to them!" He trod his feet down in the new boots. Leather creaked. "Because I'll shortly ride a horse foaled by an acorn. Let's not keep them waiting. Have you money about you?"

Sir John Hay shook his head. "Not a farthing."

"Furies. Attend. Gadsbury has my voice for captain." He rested his arm across Arbella Lacey's shoulders as they walked, sparing a glance backward for the small dark man, staggering and supported between Linebaugh and Thompson. "Tell him so when he's sober."

The redheaded woman cuffed a prison brat aside. She rubbed the mud-stain left on her old kid glove. Brocade breeches and coat embroidered with silver plate and sequins flashed in the barred sunlight. From polished heeled boots to plumed broad-brimmed hat, the woman strode with a mercenary's brittle vanity.

"The company won't be the same. Do you remember Parry, at Aqua Sulis?" Reflective memory of the dead captain clear on her face. "Damn, there was a shit-stupid man. *Attack through the sewers, men, we can take the town!* And us with a comfortable seige there to see us out the whole summer, if we nursed it along."

"Not to mention petard mines in the sewer-system. I remember."

His stride outdistanced her under the stone arch, exiting into the open, bitter-cold prison yard. He all but ran into a man coming in the other direction.

"Sir." The man removed his plumed hat with some deliberation. Black hair straggled either side of a long, sallow face; his sharp chin made sharper by a small, pointed beard. Tan-and-cream brocade hung loosely on him as if his long coat had been made for a larger man.

"Phillip Nashe." A cultured voice. He held out a strong-fingered hand. "Queen's Hangman."

Pollexfen Calmady, dry-handed, returned the grip. He took in the weather-worn face, the expression somewhere between shabbiness and pride; summing him up shortly. "Captain Yates's—no, Captain Huizinga's troop?"

"Some four years since. I took orders Lammastide last."

The priest-hangman drew a notepad from his waistcoat pocket and made notes with a charcoal-stick, glancing up, practised eye measuring height, weight, drop.

Cold air grazed Calmady's newly shaven chin. He rubbed one cheek.

The straggle-haired man smudged calculations with a dirty thumb, frowned and nodded. He indicated the cart and two yoked dray-horses by the gate. An elderly man in a white shirt already stood in the tumbril. "I ride with you."

Calmady walked beside Nashe toward the tumbril and the prison-gates. The swarthy man limped slightly.

"There are good deaths and bad deaths, we know that." Pollexfen Calmady spoke quietly; businesslike. "Shot in the stomach; thirst; half your face blown off by some sapper's mine; cancerous gangrene; well . . ."

Phillip Nashe's bearded chin jutted, indicating the scattering of black-coated men and women among the yard's crowds. "Yes, and Tower Hill, your entrails and privates hacked out and burned, before the axe. That would have been Protectorate justice, Captain Calmady."

Calmady's features twisted into a momentarily uncontrollable expression. His gloved hand pressed into the bottom of the new coat's pocket. A handful of metal circlets bruised his fingers. Relief, sudden and startling, sang in his blood.

"True enough, sir. Your business, now, is to tie a knot well, so matters expedite as quick as may be."

The sovereigns slipped from his gloved fingers to the man's hand.

"You shall have a good knot. I shall have your coat and small-clothes too, or the compensation for that prerequisite." Nashe prodded the small heap of gold coins in his palm, and thrust them deep into his pocket. "And Queen's Bounty.

Sir, I'm obliged to ask what peace you've made, and how, and in what mind you're like to die."

Shabby, dark-eyed, the priest's gaze by reason of his shorter stature fell below Calmady's face. Calmady shrugged.

"I'm caught between her Majesty and the bitch-General; a cause I've risked my life for, on either side. *Non sum qualis eram:* today I am a different man. It's a fine irony that I should be brought here to make my peace with God."

Reverberate echoes from the cold masonry yard waked shivers between his shoulder-blades. Open, sunny skies blazed over the prison roofs. Wooden steps set at the back of the prison-cart sparkled, treacherous with frost. He halted.

"Captain. Here."

He took a bottle from Lord Rule. His throat moved as he tilted his head back and drank, pale skin exposed to the winter sunlight. Another shiver walked the bones of his back.

Gadsbury's head lifted. "*Regina* Carola, damn her."

"The Queen and her Hangman." Rough brandy scoured his mouth. Pollexfen Calmady coughed. He pulled Gadsbury into a bear-hug, the stink of stale vomit and brandy hitting him in the face.

"Do you carry all your brains in your arse? Go broke on brandy now and how will you live out the winter?" He shook the small man roughly. "Man, I remember you drinking! The night I lost the last of Calmady Estate on the turn of two cards. *Go for a soldier now*, you said, *or go be a thief.* We chose well enough."

"You never would cheat at cards."

"It brings me to this reckoning at the last."

He squinted at the early afternoon sun, westering; turned his face briefly into the east wind. Brandy blurred vision. The wooden steps knocked his feet, swinging himself up into the cart. Phillip Nashe banged the tailgate up; the elderly man—*T* branded already on his forehead—vomited a small pool of liquid onto the straw on the jolting planks.

The tension of his shoulders against the cold loosened. He stretched his head up. Winter sun, warm now that the cart rumbled out of the prison gates and the wind, slanted across his face. A deep breath escaped him.

Deep, felt through belly and the pit of his bowels, the tumbril wheels scraped straw-covered cobbles. Iron wheel-rims struck sparks and children darted back. The constant noise of shouting filled his hollow chest, effervescent; so that he bowed to either side, with a conscious style, smiling as the puppets in the convent-garden booths smile.

Every tavern in Holborn, every inn and every gin-shop spilled their customers out into the slush-deep road. Men and women crowded around the slowly moving cart. He leaned down to clasp hands with a dozen, two dozen; lifted his hat to acknowledge cheers. Hundreds of bobbing heads dizzied him crowding the road ahead. He lifted his gaze to snowy roofs, to the street's windows, casements open despite the cold. Red-cheeked women cheered.

A yellow-haired girl leaned out to toss a bright object, fluttering down. He caught it from the air: a red rose, folded and cut from rosewater-coloured paper, bright against the winter white. He bowed, and removed his hat to fix the paper flower into the silver-lace band.

Winter cold bit his fingertips through his white gloves. The shadow of St. Sophia's steeple momentarily fell cold on his face.

Children bundled in black rags ran along beside the cart. A stone rattled from the wood. He lifted his head. Every snow-ledged tenement window here stood jammed with black-clad men and women, white faces solemn, none shouting, none cheering.

Pollexfen Calmady took off his hat and held it to his breast, and bowed ceremoniously. Aware of how the skirts of his coat swung, flashing sunlight from silver trimming; how bright the paper rose gleamed against his bridal finery. He smiled as he straightened.

A sharp stone stung his hand. He did not flinch.

Bells clanged a muffled scale, tumbledown-notes: sound smashing the air, scattering up flocks of lean rooks and pigeons. The cart rumbled under the eaves of St. Giles in the Fields. Deafened, he threw his head back and laughed into the sea-wild, shaking air.

The White Crow hung on, balancing on the coach's outside step, snow-wet air reddening her fingers. The sword-hilt jabbed her hip. Her tone provoked.

"It's *your* area of expertise, sir, after all. Didn't you publish *On the Circulation of the Blood?*"

Sir William Harvey peered out irritably between the blind and the window-frame of the coach. "So must I have the Invisible College study a *magia* of the gallows?"

"Of course it's a *magia*. It's death without spilling blood."

One heel on the outside step, the White Crow balanced leaning back against the coach's closed door, looking down across Tyburn field as she spoke. The horses plodded through the dividing crowds.

"This all patterns around blood . . ."

Her voice echoed flatly in her ears. Wind coursed the snowy fields. Makeshift booths crammed the paths, deserted now as people in their hundreds pressed down the slope towards the gallows platform. White copses gleamed in the distance. Men and women in bright, patched cloaks trod straw into the snow: fairground-rutted.

"I came home to Roseveare: that's family blood-ties. There's the eye of the sun's blood-sacrifice. Carola's diseased blood-royal. Spilled blood, the war. The demons. Hot blood: the acts of passion. And innocent blood."

Her teasing tone vanished. She turned her head sideways to catch sight of the man's face.

"No . . . No. What it comes down to is what he did and what I did."

Wind whipped at her braids. The coach stopped some ten yards from the gallows in a press of bodies. Horse snorted; the driver tied up the reins.

William Harvey put a white-gloved hand up to block his cheek from daylight. Disguising shadow moved across his features. He muttered acerbically, "It's cost me six shillings for this coach, and a shilling each for men to help carry a body. Where's your giant—what's his name—Baltazar Casaubon?"

She rubbed at a full breast, cupping her hand over her doublet. "With Jared and the baby."

"You've left a man like that to protect your children? He looked nothing of a swordsman to me."

"To tell you the truth, he *isn't* much good with a sword. He's not built for it. It's like asking him to play tennis with a knitting-needle. Now if we still had battle-axes . . ." She chuckled, breath huffing the bitter air. "The times I've seen him in a fight, he's usually hit someone with the nearest blunt object. Last time it was a seven-foot, six-inch mahogany dining-table."

"I see." William Harvey blinked bead-black eyes.

"If I thought anyone could touch my baby I'd . . ."

"And Guillaime? The woman was something to you, you say. And you're trying to free her murderer?"

"I said once, *I hurt her.* Maybe this is to spite her. She dared to die. But I think . . ." The White Crow grinned fiercely. One hand hooked into the coach's door handle; she reached up for the iron grip to pull herself up to the roof. ". . . I *know* I've stopped caring why. I'll give you the signal. Be ready."

Houses gave way to open fields. Mothers held up children for the touch of his hand.

Bobbing heads and backs stretched out in front of the cart. Tall, rickety galleries jutted up in the fields where two roads crossed: south to Edgware, west to Oxford. Pennants unfolded into the cold wind. He gripped the cart-rail. Bright-painted coaches, shabby in this amnesty season, crowded the flat ground by the scaffold; coachmen swearing as they sought to walk the horses against the cold, or else cover them in thick blankets.

His head jolted up. He stared across milling crowds: royal-ist colour and Protectorate black, focussed on one face.

The woman sat on a level with him, on the roof of a stationary coach. Her booted feet dangled down. Tan hose, brown leather breeches and doublet, with the studs glinting silver in the afternoon sunlight; a cloak bundled up where she sat. One tan-sallow hand, uncovered, pushed at her cin-namon hair.

"I had her *twice*, you cunt!" He slammed his fist down on the cart-rail, voice booming. "She'd be a better fuck dead than you would living!"

Cold or spite whitened Valentine Roseveare's face, drew it into a scrunched contraction of eyes and mouth. Her arms folded about her thin body. Stubborn, silent, she held her-self aloof from the men and women who shrieked drunkenly around the coach and team of four. The horses stamped.

The note of wheels changed, from cobbles' hardness to snow, trodden to ice and covered with thrown-down bales of straw. He gripped the rail again as the cart lurched from side to side. The old man moaned, stinking of fear and excre-ment. Phillip Nashe murmured compassionate, inaudible words.

Tyburn's three-legged mare stood stark against sun and sky.

Stripped chestnut, knocked solidly together with iron nails—three upright posts, set at the points of a triangle, and three crossbars connecting them. The platform at the height of a man's head. Two old-and-rotted ends of rope hung down from the nearer crossbar, the ends cut and frayed and weathered.

The cart rocked, halted. Nashe leaped down, joined by his bearded assistant. Pollexfen Calmady stared up at the sky. Used to waiting, used to delays and substitutions; hear-ing finally the noise that four or five thousand men and women make. He lowered his gaze. Two more white hem-pen ropes dangled from the wood, each knotted into a noose.

He climbed down from the cart, planks chill against him,

as Phillip Nashe hurried back across the straw-covered slush; and walked up the wooden steps to the platform. The elderly thief staggered behind, the hangman's arm under his, holding him up.

One trap swung to and fro, creaking, open.

The bearded assistant stepped back to haul it up. Pollexfen Calmady stared down from the platform at the front row of the crowd. Forty or so gentlemen-mercenaries of other companies reeled, drunken, at the elbows of his own troop. Lacey, Rule, Gadsbury, Linebaugh . . . one face missing. Pissdrunk; all their gear furbished up new for the spring campaign.

A harvest field of faces beyond; hundreds, perhaps thousands for this one of the year's eight hanging-days; some heads turned aside, talking; some chewing, shouting; vendors threading paths to sell hot chestnuts; young men and women clinging to the sides of makeshift stands; all taut, wild, anticipating.

"Listen to me, my children."

He raised his voice, pitching it to carry beyond the company. Quiet spread. He jerked his head at the branded old man vomiting over Phillip Nashe's arm.

"I am brought here with another, who is to hang after me, and you see what a sorry spectacle he is. Shortly I shall hang with him—and then you shall see a pair of spectacles."

Crowd-laughter hissed: breath whitening the air, rising in the cold afternoon. His shoulders lifted, his spine straightening. Pollexfen Calmady: gruff-voiced, haranguing.

"We say, wedding and hanging go by destiny . . . Here am I dressed in white, come to make a hanging-match with my bride. Commonly a man is stiff after the wedding ceremony, and certainly this day I shall be stiff after mine."

Two or three dozen men cheered among the laughter. Pollexfen Calmady held up a gloved hand.

"You all know I hang for congress with a young woman, afterwards dead. She met the same death then that I meet now. And since it is because of her that I die, you may truly say when you see me: here hangs a man who died for love."

Cold wind whipped his cheek, carrying their flood of sound to ebb and to high-tide. Exhilarated, he planted his fists on his hips.

"I am brought here today to make a match. The bride has a something wooden look to her. Her embraces commonly prove fatal. Perhaps that is why the wedding-bells ring so dolefully yonder. I've heard it said: gain a wife and lose a life. So all take heed and love your single life while you have it."

He swallowed. Cold air drying his throat, he reached a hand down and took the bottle that Gadsbury tossed up; drank, acknowledged the raw, baying cheer with a lift of that bottle, and threw it back.

Phillip Nashe stepped forward. "You do them the honour of a good ending. They only want to see you kick on air and turn black now."

"Let 'em wait one more minute." He drew breath. The same pit-stomach fear and excitement attendant on massacres after battles shone on the faces below the platform. Raucous shouts assaulted from all sides, prompts, suggestions; filling his sudden silence.

"I see the hangman hankers to his trade, to make me one flesh with the cold clay, so I'll delay no longer. It is no groom's privilege to come late to his own wedding, and I fear this bride will not grant me that favour herself. But you may see, in plain view, the wedding-ring provided, although I'll wager it's a close fit."

Clotted humanity filled up the spaces between coaches and stands, bare-headed or with hats pulled down against the cold, men and women with breath steaming; forgetting now that they carried bottles of spirit or hot pasties and chestnuts, mouths gaping, all their eyes on him.

The noose, stark against the sky, danced at the edge of his vision. Phillip Nashe reached up. Calmady stretched out his arms.

"I am not come here to marry but to die. I come in this suit because, led into gross errors as I have been, this is the day that makes me white and clean. This is my soul's wedding day, wed with grace and justice and Judgement. And in the marriage bed I go to, I lay down with righteousness and I rise up with mercy. Of this, I have certain assurance!"

Hemp rope scratched his cheek, its stiff strands drawing blood from skin fragile in the bitter air. Arms clamped around his shoulders and biceps.

Phillip Nashe nodded, shooting a glance past his head to the assistant; his sallow hands stretching the noose with calm deliberation. Pollexfen Calmady jerked his head back.

"I'm not finished!"

The two men grabbed: he wrenched from side to side.

"No!"

The hangman's arms passed under his flailing arms. Strong-fingered hands locked across the back of his neck. His scalp stung suddenly cold, periwig knocked off and kicked down from the platform, trodden into the slush. He struggled, dragged bodily back from the Tyburn ladder. Jeers and stones and snow flew.

"No! Please!"

Wood slammed the side of his face. A long splinter jabbed his lip. He slumped against Nashe, stunned, pain a solid taste of copper in his mouth.

Tears leaked from his eyes. The wind from the north cut across the fields through white coat and shirt to shivering flesh; scalded his bare, shaved head.

"*No!*"

He shouted, bewildered, spittle flying; the two men gripping his body and dragging him back, heels hacking the frost-slippery planks. Bladder and bowel let go and he soiled himself.

"Please, I'm not ready! *Please, don't kill me!*"

Scarlet: scarlet at the edge of vision: a boy whose yellow curls fall to the shoulders of an over-large red coat, who wears an apprentice-surgeon's sash; standing whitefaced among a crowd on a knoll—

His eyes lock with the boy's. Bevil Calmady.

* * *

The White Crow hacked her heel twice on the coach roof: hollow impacts. She slid rapidly on heels, buttocks, and one hand; scabbarded sword clamped up under one arm; and let herself down off the back of the coach and into the saddle of the hired brown mare. Her gloved fingers fumbled the rein's cold straps.

She swore, hooked the second mount's reins over her saddlehorn, and lay leather across the mare's neck. The mount plodded sluggishly into the crowd. Men and women backed without looking, all their attention on the gallows-tree.

The beast's body rocked her: she clamped her knees tight. Over heads, bare or wearing low-crowned and wide-brimmed hats, the ragged plumes of the gentlemen-mercenaries bobbed. She felt in her breeches' pocket, drew her arm back, and skimmed a pebble accurately.

It struck her target. She dipped her hand. The cloak's hood fell forward. She glanced back over her shoulder. The coach-blind snicked up to disclose Sir William Harvey's powdered hair and small face.

"Surgeons!"

Gadsbury's voice: hoarse with outrage and brandy. The mare backed a pace, another pace; the crowd surged, one man swore, and a child shrieked. Rule's shocked voice bellowed: "Surgeons! Anatomists!"

Bright metal gleamed: rose, dropped. A flurry of screams and shouting went up. People jerked back from the mercenaries.

She wrapped the spare mount's reins around her right hand, backing the mare away. Arbella Lacey stumbled, threw an arm across the Margrave Linebaugh's shoulder; both forcing through the press towards Harvey's coach. The coach began to back. A high voice screamed. One man, two, a dozen: all backing and pushing.

Level now with the gallows platform, she raised her eyes to Tyburn's three beams: stark against the blue, hazed sky. The White Crow leaned forward and took a long-barrelled

pistol from the saddle-holster. Bodies banged against her
legs. The mare whickered. The gunsight, soot-black, bobbed
as she sighted along her arm: fired.

Concussion deafened. Her arm and hand stung.

Chips of wood spanged off the back of the coach.

"Surgeons!"

"Bodystealers!"

She heaved on the mare's mouth. The horse swung, pressing against the solid body of people, head tossing; hooves
shifting uneasily on slush and straw.

Crowd-pressure broke, one woman pushing past, a clear
space, men running; ten yards away the coach dipped over
with a scream of wood, one high wheel in a rut; whipshots
from the carrier: the team heaving free, clattering, the coach
bouncing up; fifty, a hundred men and women running towards it.

"*Riot!*"

The White Crow raised her head. Frost-dark steps went
up beside her. Her knee banged the edge of the wooden
platform painfully. Silhouetted against the sky, two men
held Calmady in a straining, solid grip. A hemp loop swung.

The elderly, branded man slipped down from the platform's far side; threw himself into the crowd, vanished.

"*—arrest in the Queen's na—*"

Screams and shouts deafened. Officers with staves spurred
down towards William Harvey's coach, hard on its way to
Oxford Street. She sat calmly in the frosty air; the taste of
gunpowder sour on her lips. Women and men running in
pursuit, arms flailing; stones curving across the bright sky;
the smash of breaking wood, children squalling.

A short-haired girl of twelve screamed, pushed up against
the platform steps. The White Crow locked eyes with her.

The child's mouth squared, screaming; tears ran down her
dirty face.

"Help me!"

The White Crow dug heels into the mare's side, pushing
the barrel-body against the mass of women and men; easing

pressure on the trapped girl. "Help for help. Give me your hand."

"Help *meee*—"

"Your hand: *now.*"

Seconds or minutes? Bobbing heads hid the vanishing coach; staves rose and fell towards Oxford Street. In the open spaces men and women milled about, shouting. She jumped at another shot, stark across the afternoon cold.

The two men held Pollexfen Calmady bent over double. The blond-bearded man twisted both of Calmady's arms up behind his back; the dark, smaller man wrested the hemp rope over his shaved head; made a grab for the trap-lever.

Seconds. The White Crow grinned, fierce, riding it; riding the cessation of time that comes with action; all the time in the world now, if everything's done on the instant, and so—

Sir William Harvey and the decoy coach drawing off crowds, the riot well in progress, she leaned forward again to the open saddle bags. Paper rustled as she moved. A thin strip of parchment, inked over with hastily written sigils, wound around her wrist and thumb, pinned with a silver pin.

With that hand she drew out a greasy playing-card.

The winter sunlight gleamed on the oblong of pasteboard. Pale inks delineated the old image. A spear, whose iron tip bleeds stylised droplets of blood. Below the head, the dead wooden shaft sprouts a small green leaf. *Ace of Lances.*

"I would do this myself."

She edged the mare between bodies and gallows-steps. The yellow-haired girl in layers of black rags bawled square-mouthed, deep shuddering breaths racking her with hysteria. The White Crow leaned down from the saddle, grabbed one of the hands that clamped across her face, and dug her fingers in hard.

"Ow!" The girl yelled.

"I would do this myself, but I'm going to need both hands later. Hold this. No: *hold it.* Trust me."

A shaking, chilblained hand gripped the card.

The White Crow pressed the small hand against the side

of the gallows-steps, the Ace of Lances flattened between the girl's palm and the wood. She reached behind to her left hip, drew her Italian stiletto, positioned it, and slammed the thin blade down between bone and tendon.

"*Aaahhhhh!*"

Screams ripped out of the child's throat. Her free hand lashed the horse's belly, clawed White Crow's boot. All around her eyes the skin showed fish-belly white. Shrieks split the air.

The White Crow put two fingers against the back of the child's hand, dabbling in the trickle of blood. She drew three short strokes on the wooden rail of the steps. She gripped the girl's wrist, took the stiletto out with one pull, and slammed the knife back to pin the blood-stained card to the wood.

A hard jerk shifted her in the saddle; she let go the child's wrist as the girl's teeth met in her hand; wrenched her gloved flesh away, swearing; and half-slipped, one foot losing a stirrup.

Screaming, sobbing, in shock, the child fell back into the churned slush under the wooden steps.

The White Crow sat back hard in the saddle. Her chilled foot found the stirrup, boot-toe knocking against the wooden framework of the steps. She shifted her sword and scabbard to lay across her lap. Wet straw, cordite, and urine: the air stank.

"Calmady!"

Bitter wind cut between her cloak-hood and ruff. The hood slipped down. She brought her left hand up to her teeth, tugging off the thick glove. The glove fell to the ground, the mare trampling it among discarded food, broken plumes, a lost shoe. The wind brought tears trickling from the corners of her eyes.

She leaned forward and spat. Saliva spattered the pinned card, trickling across the wet blood and the ink image. Barehanded, she smudged the sigil's final line.

Wood creaked.

A scent drifted across her nostrils. All the muscles in her
back relaxed. She sat easy in the saddle, the scent of cut
grass in the wind.

The cold air shimmered.

A furnace-blast of heat hit. The mare's head lifted; the
spare mount neighed and threw up its head, jerking the rein
tied to the saddle-horn. Timber groaned, creaked, as ships
do in deep waters, as woods do in a high wind.

The split, stripped chestnut darkened.

Green pinpoints ran the length of the step-rail, spread
onto the platform, spread under the feet of Pollexfen Calmady and the Queen's Hangman and the hangman's assistant; green specks budding into knots of lime-colour,
unfurling into tiny, pale-green leaves; sprouting, green nubs
rising and lengthening, and the folded-down new leaves un-
folding umbrella-upwards into the palmate sprays of chestnut foliage.

She plunged her arms across the edge of the platform into
twigs. New wood scratched her skin, her face. The White
Crow stood up in the stirrups; shouting, wordless, wild.

The blond-bearded assistant leapt back. His legs and feet
lifted, no sooner touching the impossible leaves but he
leaped up again; staggering back, mouth widely open, yelling; he fell from the back of the gallows platform. His body
thudded down into straw.

"*Calmady, damn you!*"

The Queen's Hangman, arms above his head, wrestled
white hemp rope down.

Fibres split, greening, twining; winding tendrils up
against the hazed blue sky. Sweat and effort reddened the
man's cheeks. The rope, unwoven, living grass, fell apart in
his hands.

"Calmady! *Here!*"

The Queen's Hangman stood among sprouting twigs, all
the platform a mass of five-fingered chestnut leaves. Each
upright post twisted, new brown bark wrinkling across it;

green shade dappled from the crossbeams, rustling with thick foliage. The hangman slowly began to strip off his tan-and-white long coat, standing in his shirt-sleeves.

The White Crow wiped sweat from her cheeks.

The mare whickered, lifting mobile lips and nostrils to scent at the new leaves. Its brown eyes rolled. The spare mount, a large-boned grey gelding, dipped and shook its head, uneasy. She unknotted the reins from the saddle-horn.

Swearing, his white coat catching and ripping on stout twigs, Pollexfen Calmady thrashed to the edge of the gallows platform.

The cold straps crumpled in her fist. She leaned up and threw the reins of the spare mount. He dropped to his knees among sprouting green leaves, big-knuckled hands scrabbling. Winter sun slanted among leaves. Silver lace and brocade blazed.

The curling wig gone, his shaved head exposed, Calmady's features stood out with brutal emphasis. Afternoon light shadowed deep creases around his nose and mouth. His ears jutted, prominent against his cropped scalp; muscles shifted across the breadth of his shoulders and back.

"Move!" She reined in, backing the mare.

Pollexfen Calmady lurched forward, belly-down across the gelding's saddle. He swung powerful legs up; his white breeches and coat now green-stained. Sweat trickled down his face. He panted. He reached across and ripped a chestnut switch from the new wood; buttocks firmly in the saddle, knees gripping; and slashed the gelding's haunches.

The White Crow wheeled, hacked heels into the mare's ribs, bowled two men over, galloping on uncertain ground, new icy wind slapping her face; all surprise, all speed, all instant flight.

XII

The gallows posts root.

Canopies of leaves lift from three new, rooted chestnut trees. The winter light through their leaves is pale, all the bright colours of green made into a fineness as of stained glass.

Staves thunk down across heads, shoulders, raised arms; sheriff's officers riding hard across the wake of the coach that now swings into the first houses and alleys off Oxford Street, the acerbic man clinging to the interior handgrips, swearing all the way.

A woman kneels, face stretched in a mask of pain, cradling a broken arm. Arbella Lacey squats down to help, ripping her brocade coat, that is smeared with slush and horse-dung, to use as an impromptu sling.

Two men carry a hurdle: on it, the trampled body of a third.

In the shadow of a platform become roots, a twelve-year-old girl curls up foetally, squalling; her mouth pressed to the back of her hand. Blood drips and soaks her black, torn coat.

A last breath of green warmth drifts over Tyburn fields.

*   *   *

"Did you enjoy it, the second time you had her, sober?"

Pollexfen Calmady eased in the saddle.

"Yes."

"Were you sorry when she died?"

His face creased into an expression of contagious irony. "When it seemed I should die to atone for it, I was repentant. Now that it seems I'll live, I find myself growing reconciled to the fact."

"Ride."

She said no other word for fifteen minutes. No noise but the beat of hooves on frozen ground, hard riding, and the whip of leafless branches to avoid: voices shouting, a distant shot.

"*Now.*"

She swung into cover in a copse at the edge of the Park. Dirty snow clung to trunks and twigs. Ahead, smoke breathed from chimneys. Her cheeks ached with the grin that, do what she would, stayed on her face.

"Leave the hired hacks to find their way back to the stables."

She took Pollexfen Calmady's shoulder in her hand as he dismounted and came to peer out from cover.

"It'll be seen fast enough that snow keeps us from leaving town." Her fingers dug into the white cloth of his coat. "And so we must have turned back into town, which we have; and for the next I count on their thoughts running in an old track. Which is, that all criminals and fugitives take refuge in the stews of Northbankside, and to that there's but one way: the only bridge across Thamys, at Southwark."

The big man blinked dazed eyes. "They'll have set guards on the bridge by now and we're four miles away. Do we steal a boat—"

The White Crow turned her head so that her braids flew, cold hair stinging her cheeks. She shook him gently.

"All the Thamys is a bridge now! Ten minutes directly north of here, at Westminster, we can cross the ice and be in Northbankside, safely lost."

* * *

The Protector looked up from her desk at Humility Talbot. "We have six who claim bastardy by the godless woman's father." Talbot folded his hands together against the Tower room's chill.

"Try their blood separately over the next six days. Omitting the sabbath, of course." Olivia turned back to her papers. It became apparent that the man waited. She lifted bulbous, placid features.

"General." Humility Talbot protested. "You know my skill in architecture is scant. Too much knowledge of the Black Art of Geometry corrupts the soul. But even I can tell that a temple consecrated with bastard blood is no temple but an abomination!"

"A temple is a temple," Olivia said tranquilly. "I have no intention, neither, of letting the godless woman Carola use a failure of ours as steps to her own success. Do as I order."

The last, said kindly, brought a flush to his pale cheeks.

"Take these as you go." She held out a scroll of plans. Visible on one edge, neat inkwork lettered: ST. SOPHIA REBUILDING PROJECT. "They'll serve to kindle a fire in the outer room."

Breath burned in her lungs, chest tight from exertion. The White Crow ran across herb-gardens, their surfaces nothing but lumpy snow; the paths' deep mud frozen and crackling under her boots. She leaped a fence to the embankment and ducked into a jetty's shelter.

Blue sky, fire-coloured to the west, spread out in a huge arc. Tall, tilted houses looked down on a slope that, in summer, would be stinking mud; the jutting piers and steps weed-shrouded. Now foot-tracked snow covered the banks and abandoned wherries of the Thamys.

Spars of wood and thrown bricks starred the ice that, ridged and rippled and deeper than the houses' height, gleamed black under the crusting snow. Voices rasped her nerves with their nearness.

Deliberately, she did not look back. Running the risk on the knife-edge, aware, alert; the White Crow smiled as Pollexfen Calmady plodded through knee-deep snow and into the jetty's shelter.

"Northbankside."

Five hundred yards distant, across flat and exposed ice, the clustered tenements smudged the winter air with smoke. A little downriver the spires of Lambeth Palace jutted up. She cast a glance back over her shoulder. A mess of tiny alleys ran down from Westminster to the river houses here.

"It was as well, perhaps, to dress in white." She slid the leather cloak from her shoulders, reversing it to show the undyed wool lining. "You—"

Almost forgotten: who stands beside her. Almost forgotten, almost taken to be one of the Scholar-Soldiers who, in other days, shared other escapes. The shock of seeing his creased, sweating face made her head sing.

The gentleman-mercenary looked up at the sky.

She snarled. "Damn, there used not to be sentries at Westminster but I don't know now: *move!*"

The winter sun shone on his shaved head, skin blotched red and blue with cold. He took three strides down onto the embankment, staring across the frozen river. Hurriedly she swung the cloak about her shoulders and followed.

His shoulder struck her a glancing blow.

She swore, staggered ankle-deep in fresh snow; grabbed to steady herself, and fell straddling a broken oar, frozen into the mud.

The big man sprawled on his knees, his head bowed. *"Have mercy upon me, O God, according to thy loving-kindness: according unto the multitude of thy tender mercies blot out my transgressions."*

His bass voice boomed, resonant.

"Oh, Lord." The White Crow wrenched her knee and leg out of the snow, shivering, and slipped down beside him. "Now's a fine time to think of the Hanging Psalm. *Captain!*"

Metal scraped scabbard.

A glimpse of blue cloth against blackened timbers: the tall soldier in redingote and plumed hat strode out of one alley. Cavalry boots crunched slush. His long sabre sliced sunlight. She in that one instant caught his eyes, bright with cold, registering the kneeling man all in white. The soldier opened his mouth, beard rimed with frozen breath.

"Hold! I arrest you in the Queen's name!"

She appeared to stumble, rising from beside the kneeling man; drew her sword a fraction of a moment after the soldier raised his; stepped forward to engage and threw the handful of gathered ice into his eyes. She parried his thrust away one-handed, metal showering sparks; bashed his blade down; recovered a two-handed grip on her hilt and chopped an axe-blow up at his throat.

Explosive: hot, salt-wet liquid splashed her face and breast and shirt. She dripped red. His body's weight pulled her forward. She braced, tugging the blade back, wrist jarred by contact with jaw and skull-bones. He slumped awkwardly on the frozen bank, head fallen back. Pierced jugular spouted rhythmically, dying to a dribble.

Hot wetness chilled. She coughed, choking on the butcher's-shop stink. She pulled her doublet and shirt away from her body, wiped hopelessly at her breeches.

Blood dried taut on her skin.

She knelt and cleaned her blade on the dead man's lace ruffles. His body cooled.

Snow, melted in her hands, ran red. She rinsed her face. The chill cut bone-deep. She wiped her boots with handfuls of snow, dabbed at stained shirt and abandoned the idea; and straightened to face the cold wind and the bright sun.

More distant voices: urgent.

She stooped again and went through the soldier's pockets. Empty. A farthing lurked in the last, among fluff; she held it for a second and then threw it down to sparkle, bronze, on his chest.

His wig tipped back off his head into the snow; disclosing a young face, a scalp furred with baby-fine stubble.

Every muscle shaking, she turned. Pollexfen Calmady stood, barely risen to his feet. Blood soaked into the slush-ridged embankment. She guided the tip of her blade to the sheath with her other hand and snicked it home.

"Deliver me from blood-guiltiness, O God, thou God of my salvation—" Light moved on his face between his nose and cheek. The tear ran down and dropped. Calmady bent and picked up the dead soldier's sabre. He shouldered past the White Crow, boots skidding as he crabbed down the river bank to the ice.

"I had as soon he'd lived. It was too sudden and I too unsure."

Her words lost themselves flatly in stinging cold air. She snatched up her cloak, bundled it over her reddened clothes; scrambling for the Thamys ice with the sound of other sentries' calls echoing behind.

"Why should we run, go into exile?" The swarthy woman smiled. "Will you not fight for us if we stay?"

More soberly than one might have expected, Sir Denzil Waldegrave said, "Men will fight for your Majesty. Not win—the rebellious forces are too strong. But not entirely lose either. Bloody battles if you stay, madam."

"Would you have us abandon our father's kingdom?"

Carola laughed, lazily, and rolled over among silk sheets and ruffled the boy's hair. Denzil avoided his son's eyes, glimpsing that young man's nakedness under the cloth.

"We have it in mind to hold a masque."

He frowned. "Excellent device, your Majesty, had we but the money."

"A masque . . . upon Thamys, we think, the while it remains frozen. We will have the ice carven into fantastic shapes, and ways to bring fires out into midriver without danger—to moor balloons, perhaps, and suspend fires from them? And then to feast there, we think, a week and more; and then to hold the masque with such costumes, jewels, paint, and musicianry as was never seen before . . . The

scenery itself carved from ice! Commission young poets to
write it."

Sir Denzil Waldegrave lifted his comfit-box and selected
a sweetmeat. He stared past the swarthy woman, through
the window, towards the sun on the frozen river.

"As your Majesty desires. I . . . forgive me, these poets,
cooks, bakers, mechanics; all will demand hard coin. There's
no more credit to be had in this city. I tried for that when
it came to refurbishing the ordnance for this spring."

Regina Carola chuckled deep in her throat.

"We have the money. What, man, don't look so amazed.
We are this land's monarch, and some are loyal still . . .
We have six thousand guineas. We will devise this masque
ourselves. Now hurry! And it shall be called—yes—*The
Masque of the Contention between Abstinence and Desire.*"

Walls of frozen snow bashed her shoulders as she stumbled
down the narrow, lumpy corridor. The sky made a pale rib-
bon above her head. Deep trenches crisscrossed the
Thamys: footpaths worn down and buttressed up through
the snow that, where untouched, lay the height of a man
on top of the river's black ice.

The edge of the inside-out cloak hood rasped her cheek.
The White Crow scratched at her face with fingers whose
nails were rimmed brown-red. The cold numbed hands,
face, feet. Rounded ice betrayed her steps. She staggered,
shoulders tense.

Pollexfen Calmady's breath echoed in the trench behind
her. She spared one glance to see that he kept his head
down. The brief sight showed her no glimpse of the far-
distant bank, invisible above the ice-trenches. She must assume soldiers outdistanced and Northbankside scant yards
ahead.

"Here!"

The trench shallowed, opening up ahead of her. Late sun,
pure and clear as honey, shone on the backs of tenement
houses. Practised, her eye picked out the safe path to them,

the path in cover—from concealing trench to pier to walled
river bank, where frost-damaged masonry sprawled in
collapse.

"Even if they can cross, that's useless to them. This place
is a maze! But wait."

She moved up a few yards, crouching in the shelter of
the shallow trench, the trodden-down snow giving under
her. A glance behind showed Westminster distant and deserted. For a moment no cold seeped through. Her breath
feathered the air. A breathing, warm body shouldered down
beside her. She gazed up, taking him in from slush-black-
ened boots to disarranged shirt. His lace cravat had burst
open and now trailed down his half-unbuttoned coat, his
chest heaving. A mutual campaigners' conspiracy ignored
the stink of shit.

She stared with nothing to say, almost shy: the man momentarily become again a stranger.

"I conceive it possible we'll fight now." Captain Pollexfen
Calmady handled the dead cavalryman's sabre. "No?"

"No."

"Why not?"

"Not because of Desire Guillaime. And not because of
Casaubon. And not even because I've got two children and
know your feelings for Bevil and his for you. And not because of fear."

"That last I credit. The first I don't apprehend."

She hacked one heel at the river's dirty, thick ice. Cold
gnawed at her feet and fingers and earlobes, reddened her
cheeks, fired all her blood.

Away across the white expanse behind them a tiny flame
flared. Seconds after, the shot's echo sounded. Speculative
fire. She drew the reversed cloak about her, the undyed
wool lining merging into the colours of snow. Half-dry and
half-damp shirt cloth crackled.

"Once I had to nurse a sick man in a little room. He died.
Everything outside that room seemed to fade away. We
were insulated, away from the rest of life." She shrugged.

"What goes on inside that room is pure, if you like, but it has very little to do with our decisions outside it. Being born and dying are the givens. They're what happens, that's all."

Now she smiled.

"I would be a liar *now* if I pretended that I cared for Desire Guillaime any more than you do. I have my guilt. Killing you—that would just be rank hypocrisy."

The man brushed snow from his white-dirty sleeves as one might flick away thread or ash.

"You don't know that you could kill me. I would gamble, myself. You see, I have no regrets."

She broke cover, loping towards the shelter of the pier. No shouts. His footsteps and breathing sounded at her back. She picked her way cautiously up the icy river steps and into the cover of a dockside wall, among timbered houses.

Here voices sounded from behind closed doors, the noise of song, drinking, eating; pigs in their pens grunting for scarce scraps, and the tarred bodies of malefactors hung in chains chanting their confessions. Four or five alleys led away into Northbankside's stews. And Casaubon and Jared and the baby where?

She turned her head.

"Not I—"

Only an empty river bank: Pollexfen Calmady gone.

The thirty-year-old woman scratched at her aching, full breasts, irritated by the dried blood. She stared into empty air.

Downriver.

Into a hazed white void, edged with the city. Frozen water. Whitehall's distant spires. The ragged scaffolding of the eye of the sun. And, furthest, the forest of bare masts at the docks, pointing towards the sea.

The open sea.

The last of the afternoon sun cut a bright line across chimney-stacks and snow-covered roofs. She shrugged her cloak off and reversed it to its proper side, drew her blade to carry loosely in her left hand, and walked at random into the frozen alleyways. Her steps, slow at first, quickened. Before she had gone a hundred yards she began to sing under her breath.